W9-BZN-685

PENGUIN CLASSICS

A PRINCE OF SWINDLERS

GUY BOOTHBY (1867–1905) was one of the most successful authors of crime fiction during the turn of the twentieth century. Born in Adelaide, South Australia, to a prominent Australian political family, Boothby wrote more than fifty books in a decade, before passing away at thirty-seven. Along with his stories about gentleman thief Simon Carne, Boothby published one of the earliest mummy horror stories, *Pharos, the Egyptian* (1899), as well as a series of novels featuring one of the more nefarious criminal masterminds, Dr. Nikola, in *A Bid for Fortune: or, Dr. Nikola's Vendetta* (1895), *Dr. Nikola* (1896), *The Lust of Hate* (1898), *Dr. Nikola's Experiment* (1899), and *"Farewell, Nikola"* (1901).

GARY HOPPENSTAND is a professor of English at Michigan State University. A recipient of numerous awards from the National Popular Culture Association, he is the former editor of the *Journal of Popular Culture* and recently introduced Grant Allen's *An African Millionaire* for Penguin Classics.

GUY BOOTHBY

A Prince of Swindlers

Introduction by
GARY HOPPENSTAND

PENGUIN BOOKS

PENGUIN BOOKS

Published by the Penguin Group
Penguin Group (USA) LLC
375 Hudson Street
New York, New York 10014

USA | Canada | UK | Ireland | Australia | New Zealand | India | South Africa | China
penguin.com
A Penguin Random House Company

First published in Great Britain by Ward, Lock & Co. 1900
Published in the United States of America by A. Westbrook Co. 1907
This edition with an introduction by Gary Hoppenstand published in Penguin Books 2015

Introduction copyright © 2015 by Gary Hoppenstand

ISBN 978-0-14-310722-4
CIP data available

Printed in the United States of America
1   3   5   7   9   10   8   6   4   2

Set in Sabon

Contents

Introduction

When Sir Arthur Conan Doyle attempted to kill Sherlock Holmes in the 1893 story "The Final Problem," the proposed demise of Holmes was perhaps also a symbolic death knell for the amateur detective in popular crime fiction. At that moment, the amateur detective hero was undergoing some substantial formulaic revision and was being split into two different narrative directions.

The first of these narrative directions landed in the gothic supernatural genre, where the amateur detective became the amateur occult detective. The early source of this transformational development began in the work of the Irish-born gothic writer Joseph Sheridan Le Fanu, in his collection of tales *In a Glass Darkly* (1872), published as the posthumous files of the fictitious occult investigator Dr. Martin Hesselius. Irish author Bram Stoker sculpted Le Fanu's reflective Dr. Hesselius into a fearless vampire killer in his novel *Dracula* (1897), which features an occult professor named Abraham Van Helsing, who functions as Stoker's rational voice in the story by explaining and justifying the supernatural powers of Dracula both to other characters and to the reader. English writer Algernon Blackwood continued this trend in *John Silence, Physician Extraordinary* (1908), a short story collection containing an assortment of tales that highlight a consulting occult physician as an interconnected framing device for the stories. British-born William Hope Hodgson contributed his own version of the ghost hunter in his collection *Carnacki, the Ghost-Finder* (1913), thus completing the conversion of Conan Doyle's pragmatic, hyper-rational amateur detective into the "supernatural sleuth." This character type continued through the twentieth century in the American pulp fiction magazines to the contemporary writers of urban fantasy, arguably reaching its cultural zenith in the comic mode with the 1980s film franchise *Ghostbusters*, and remaining popular today in films like *The Conjuring*.

The second narrative direction resulted in the creation of the gentleman thief protagonist, a culmination of the hero-turned-villain. Indeed, as reader interest heightened through the second half of the nineteenth century for the villain-as-protagonist, the brilliant sleuth who made fools of the professional police was no longer the detective hero, but instead the gentleman thief. While the late-Victorian occult detective was essentially a product of Irish and British writers, the gentleman thief possessed a French readership in addition to a British and American audience. The most important of the French gentleman thief protagonists was Arsène Lupin, penned by the prolific French novelist Maurice Leblanc, while the most famous, or infamous, of these British and American gentleman thief protagonists included Grant Allen's Colonel Clay, E. W. Hornung's Raffles, Frederick Irving Anderson's Infallible Godahl, and, of course, Guy Boothby's Simon Carne.

The origins of the gentleman thief protagonist in popular crime fiction began in a series of interconnected short stories featuring the master crook Colonel Clay, written by author Grant Allen and appearing in *The Strand Magazine* from June 1896 through May 1897. These stories were later collected in a book entitled *An African Millionaire*, published in 1897, interestingly the same year that Bram Stoker's *Dracula* appeared. Canadian-born Grant Allen (1848–1899) began a career as a full-time writer in 1876. Most of his early work was in the sciences, but he eventually turned to writing fiction, and between 1884 and 1899 he wrote prolifically. The only novel (or more correctly, collection of interconnected short stories) Allen wrote that continues to be read today is *An African Millionaire*. His seminal character, Colonel Clay, in addition to being a gentleman thief, was also a master of disguise (hence his professional sobriquet). He could alter his face and manners at will, fooling both the authorities and his intended target, Sir Charles Vandrift. Sir Charles, the reader quickly learns, is the African millionaire of the book's title, an obtuse man housing the capitalistic character faults of greed and stupidity, faults that, of course, left him at the mercy of the trickster Colonel Clay. Each short story in the series recounted a new scheme of Clay's to relieve Vandrift of his great wealth, employing disguise and Vandrift's greedy ambition to his successful advantage. Colonel Clay was a robber stealing from a "robber baron" figure, in essence stealing from one who steals from others.

British-born Ernest William Hornung (1866–1921), a literary contemporary of Grant Allen's in England, was a successful and prolific writer of gaslight-era melodrama and thrillers. He began his writing career as a journalist and a poet, and then later became a popular novelist. Though the majority of Hornung's literary efforts are forgotten today, the adventures of his gentleman thief protagonist, A. J. Raffles, continue to be read (and imitated in a number of pastiches by authors such as Graham Greene, Peter Tremayne, and Barry Perowne). Raffles appeared in three collections of short stories—*The Amateur Cracksman* (1899), *The Black Mask* (1901), and *A Thief in the Night* (1905)—as well as in one novel, *Mr. Justice Raffles* (1909). During the course of his ten-year career in crime, Raffles evolved from an "amateur" thief, to a professional thief, to a war hero who dies in battle during the Boer War. Hornung intended to kill off Raffles at the conclusion of *The Black Mask*, but reader demand seemingly compelled Hornung to resurrect his popular gentleman thief in the novel *Mr. Justice Raffles*, a story set before the Boer War. Raffles is thus similar to Conan Doyle's Sherlock Holmes: both characters appeared to be killed by their creators, and then were brought back to life for additional adventures by the influence of their distraught readers when economic pressure was exerted on the authors. However, unlike Raffles, who remained buried the second time around, Sherlock Holmes was revealed not to have perished at the conclusion of the tale "The Final Problem" and—following the interlude of a previous adventure recorded in *The Hound of the Baskervilles*—reappeared alive and healthy in the story "The Adventure of the Empty House."

George Orwell saw a certain virtue in Raffles. In his essay "Raffles and Miss Blandish," Orwell offers a comparison between the Raffles stories by E. W. Hornung and the James Hadley Chase novel *No Orchids for Miss Blandish* (1939). The latter does not compare favorably in Orwell's view, because it embraces the "sadistic" and "masochistic" elements found in the American pulp magazines of that era, even though Chase was a British author writing for a British audience enduring the London Blitz. Specifically, Orwell objects to the morally equivocal representation of crime in the story, where "being a criminal is only reprehensible in the sense that it does not pay." The police employ criminal methods in Chase's novel, Orwell explains, so that there is little moral difference between crook and cop. Orwell states: "This is a new departure for English sensational fiction, in which till recently there has always been a sharp distinction between right and wrong and a general agreement that virtue must triumph in the last chapter." Indeed, Raffles, along with many of the gentleman crooks and con artists coexisting with Hornung's creation, decidedly avoided the hearty strain of violence typically found in the British pulp fiction periodicals of the period, as well as in the nineteenth-century American dime novels and early twentieth-century pulp magazines that featured crime fiction.

While Grant Allen's Colonel Clay and E. W. Hornung's Raffles plundered England's elite, Frederick Irving Anderson's Infallible Godahl was the only significant American gentleman thief to appear in crime fiction in the years prior to World War I. Perhaps an American audience was less inclined to accept a morally ambivalent American protagonist in crime fiction, while simultaneously having no difficulty in reading the adventures of British and French gentleman thieves. No doubt the American readership perceived the older European culture as being more decadent, and subsequently was inclined to accept their rogues and thieves as heroes. Anderson's Infallible Godahl was featured in just six stories published in the so-called slick periodical *The Saturday Evening Post* from 1913

to 1914, which were subsequently collected in a single volume entitled *The Adventures of the Infallible Godahl* in 1914.
Though relatively unknown to today's reader, during his lifetime, American-born Frederick Irving Anderson (1877–1947)
was one of the more popular authors of thriller and detective fiction to appear in *The Saturday Evening Post*. He wrote
extensively and successfully for the slick magazine markets,
publishing more than fifty stories in *The Saturday Evening
Post* alone. He published only three volumes of crime fiction:
The Adventures of the Infallible Godahl (1914), *The Notorious Sophie Lang* (1925), and *The Book of Murder* (1930),
which the mystery writing team of "Ellery Queen" ranked as
number 82 in their "Queen's Quorum" of the 125 most important detective/crime fiction books published.

Anderson's importance as a contributor to crime fiction that
featured the gentleman thief can be found in the complex-
ity and sophistication of his plotting of the Godahl stories.
The author's touch is often subtle and complex in the series,
and Godahl's exploits may require several readings to appreciate fully the author's self-critique of literary creation, and
the broader critique of American social class, wealth, and van-
ity that frequently parallels the depiction of Godahl's amaz-
ing thefts. Anderson's work is distinguished by its descriptive
evocation of Manhattan and its surrounding environs and by
its leisurely narrative pacing, but perhaps what makes his body
of crime fiction most intriguing is his attraction to, and cel-
ebration of, the gentleman (and gentlewoman) thief. Two of
his three published books of fiction featured criminal protagonists, and he was one of the first crime fiction writers to create
a female master thief with his charismatic rogue, Sophie Lang.
Occasionally, Anderson would have his series detective heroes,
Oliver Armiston and Deputy Parr, pursue his two series villains, Godahl and Sophie Lang. But, unlike Conan Doyle having his Sherlock Holmes ultimately triumph over Professor
Moriarty, Anderson's heroes never seem to defeat their more
clever villains.

Nestled securely among these notorious gentleman and gentlewoman thief protagonists is the equally infamous Simon

Carne, the charming villain protagonist of Guy Boothby's *A Prince of Swindlers* (1900), originally serialized in *Pearson's Magazine* in 1897. Boothby was quite adept at employing villains in his fiction, and featured several in his body of work. His most famous villain protagonist was Dr. Nikola, a nefarious genius and master of the occult who appeared in a series of novels, including *A Bid for Fortune: or, Dr. Nikola's Vendetta* (1895), *Dr. Nikola* (also titled *Dr. Nikola Returns*, 1896), *The Lust of Hate* (1898), *Dr. Nikola's Experiment* (1899), and *"Farewell, Nikola"* (1901). Nikola is a visually striking and aesthetically sophisticated character, and is an important model for the cultured literary gentleman thief that soon followed. Perhaps an even more fascinating Boothby villain is Pharos, the Egyptian, featured in the 1899 novel of the same title. Pharos is, in actuality, the mummy Ptahmes, possessing magical attributes that he puts to appropriately evil use in his wicked schemes. As a prototype, *Pharos, the Egyptian* anticipates the classic Universal Studios 1932 horror film *The Mummy*, directed by Karl Freund and starring the iconic Boris Karloff (resurrected in 1999 starring Brendan Fraser). Despite this impressive cabinet of entertaining creations, Simon Carne remains Boothby's most ingenious villain, and *A Prince of Swindlers* remains one of Boothby's finest books.

As biographer Paul Depasquale notes, Guy Boothby "remains perhaps South Australia's most neglected successful author, except by antiquarians and book collectors." On October 13, 1867, in Adelaide, South Australia, Guy Newell Boothby was born to a father who served in the South Australian Legislative Assembly. After moving to England with his mother, he was educated at the Priory School in Salisbury and at Lord Weymouth's Grammar School in Warminster, Wiltshire (some sources also cite Christ's Hospital in London as another school Boothby attended). At sixteen, he returned to Australia, and with his father's and grandfather's political connections, he was hired as the private secretary to the mayor of Adelaide, Lewis Cohen, in 1890. Boothby once wrote plays, including comic operas, but although a few of these plays were produced, he failed to discover the type of success in the theater that he would eventually find as a highly prolific and popular writer of melodramatic fiction. Around 1891, Boothby traveled extensively with his friend Longley Taylor around the Pacific Islands and in the Far East.

In 1892, Boothby voyaged across the Pacific Islands region, and journeyed from Northern Queensland to Adelaide. He used these experiences in his first book, entitled *On the Wallaby; or, Through the East and Across Australia*, published in 1894. The following year, he married Rose Alice Bristowe. Also in 1895, Boothby published *A Lost Endeavour* and *The Marriage of Esther: A Torres Straits Sketch*. Besides the five Nikola adventures, Guy Boothby eventually penned more than fifty books during his brief lifetime, many of them—including *The Beautiful White Devil* (1897), *Love Made Manifest* (1899), and *The Curse of the Snake* (1902)—sensational potboilers intending to do nothing more than satisfy a voracious readership. Of his writing habits, an obituary published in the *Advertiser* noted:

> In answer to a request made by an interviewer of the *London Weekly Sun*, some time ago, Mr. Guy Boothby explained his methods of work. They were somewhat paralyzing. He got up at a fearful hour in the early dawn, when Londoners were just going to bed. His two secretaries had to be there at 5:30 a.m. He talked his novels into a phonograph, and when he had talked enough his secretaries transcribed it direct on the typewriter. ("Obituaries Australia")

Boothby's last book, *In the Power of the Sultan*, was published in 1908, three years after his death. His literary efforts brought him financial success (his earnings perhaps as high as twenty thousand pounds a year), which allowed him a well-to-do gentleman's life that involved horse breeding and book collecting. On February 26, 1905, Boothby died from influenza at the tragically young age of thirty-seven, survived by his wife, two daughters, and a son. He was buried at Bournemouth, England.

A *New York Times* obituary covering Guy Boothby's death printed this backhanded compliment about the author:

Books from his pen appeared with bewildering frequency, and among English authors it has been a standing joke that he invented a machine by which he turned them out. But, what is more to the purpose, they all sold well. The critics sneered and superior persons jeered, but the public read Boothby's novels eagerly and were always ready for more.

Though the majority of Boothby's literary efforts are forgotten by modern readers, his stories rank among the best popular crime fiction published during the turn of the twentieth century. *A Prince of Swindlers* should certainly be included in this list.

In the Preface to *A Prince of Swindlers,* Boothby establishes a clever framing device for the interconnected short stories that follow. The narrator, the Earl of Amberley, offers an embarrassed explanation to the reader, who learns that Simon Carne's spectacular series of thefts has already occurred, and that the manuscript of these adventures is intended to provide a cathartic redemption for the Earl of Amberley and his guilt at being an unwitting part of Carne's plans. The principal manuscript of *A Prince of Swindlers* is written by Carne himself, and is presented to Amberley as a mocking gift intended both to celebrate Carne's criminal accomplishments and humiliate Amberley for his gullibility. Though structured by the framing device of Amberley's reception, handling, and commentary about Simon Carne's manuscript, *A Prince of Swindlers* functions as a type of elaborate moral confession of both the triumphant con artist and the conned fool.

A Prince of Swindlers also serves as a subversive critique of the class-based economic system in late-Victorian Britain. The "brilliant season" in London that is described as the backdrop to Simon Carne's criminal exploits, the reader is told, acts as an attraction to the wealthy (and those who prey on the wealthy). The implication behind Carne's various successful schemes against London's social elite is that the privileged are a group of blithering idiots undeserving of their great wealth and privilege, because although a supposedly superior social class they are, in fact, easily duped by false appearances and insincere grace. Great wealth functions in these stories as a burden rather than as a privilege, something that can make you both a fool and a victim. By implication, in Carne's ridiculing narrative, wealth and social standing are something to be wary of; however, no practical alternative to the pursuit of wealth and social standing is ever given. Boothby's criticism is not of wealth itself, but of the incompetent upper-crust fools who mismanage the financial responsibilities of their elevated position in society.

Though Carne follows his own personal code of honor (he does not steal from Amberley, his sponsor in London society), he is nevertheless guilty of the sin of pride, as exemplified by the boastful tone in which he celebrates his deeds. The physical existence of his confessional manuscript detailing his criminal exploits is emblematic of his tremendous ego and prideful nature. One would imagine that a "professional" thief would want to attract as little attention as possible to his crimes, but for Simon Carne the success of his various schemes is apparently only part of his ambitions. He also wants to embarrass the British high society that could so easily be taken in by his acting, a performance that underscores the duality of his nature as a person and as a gentleman thief.

This duality is best represented by his physical appearance. Simon Carne masks his inward moral deformity with his hunchback disguise. By implication, then, Carne's false outward appearance of fortune and social position masks his actual, inner wicked nature. Beauty and deformity—both physical and spiritual—are transposed with each other, and ultimately become confusing to the hapless victims of Carne's schemes. Boothby, however, also employs a wonderful sense of humor with this character, as illustrated in the ironic description of Carne's portrait in the book's Preface, which offers an amusingly blunt clue about Carne's pretend physical deformity that the obtuse Earl of Amberley fails to recognize. Carne is thus having a wonderful joke on the social elite that he swindles, a knowing wink and tip of the hat that establishes a sympathetic relationship with the working-class readers of his adventures who perhaps also would like to perceive their social superiors as silly fools and buffoons.

The gentleman thief is ultimately an undermining representation of the perceived moral and social virtues of the English public (that is, private) school system, which was (and is) upper-class biased, maintaining a set of ethical standards above and apart from the working classes. Stories featuring the gentleman thief thus are the inverted mirror and moral opposite of Arthur Conan Doyle's Sherlock Holmes stories. Both Holmes and Simon Carne appeared in similar periodicals in England and America. Both were successful "amateurs" in their respective professions. But what makes this comparison between Holmes and Simon Carne even more interesting is the fact that they each represent entirely different moral stances at the turn of the twentieth century: the light and the dark, the acceptable and the unacceptable, the condoned and the outlawed that were emblematic of a Victorian worldview that was depicted in the similar literary examination of the duality of human nature found in Robert Louis Stevenson's *Strange Case of Dr. Jekyll and Mr. Hyde* (1886).

But lest the reader begin to take Boothby's commentary on London's comical social elites too seriously, with his framing-device Preface the author also layers another structuring element on Carne's sneering confessions: that of the traditional fairy tale. Note, for example, the use of the exotic, fantasy-like setting of the Indian island mansion where Amberley first encounters Simon Carne. Boothby amuses his reader at the start of the narrative by lightening the grand deus ex machina entrance of Carne in the book with what is conceivably a playful nudge at the British Empire and its governing relationship with its perceived "exotic" Indian subjects; Boothby, the well-traveled writer, brings an outsider's perspective to the British sense of imperialist superiority. This nudge and wink at the reader cautions us not to take the following events in Carne's narrative with too much gravity. The negative consequences of Carne's felonious behavior are not intended to be taken at face value. Rather, his criminal enterprises are designed to serve as an elaborate metaphor that parallels the "happy Prince" and "enchanted castle" (language employed by Boothby to describe the setting of Carne's Indian residence in the Preface) of the children's fairy tale, where important life lessons are taught, but only as a footnote to simple escapist pleasure. A fairy-tale beginning to Simon Carne's upcoming escapades softens the otherwise cruel mockery of London's privileged late-Victorian society. The book's Introduction, set in Calcutta and relating Simon Carne's conspiracy with the mysteriously sinister Trincomalee Liz, outlines for the reader his intended scheme to pilfer the "untold wealth" in London, and also reinforces this fairy-tale subtext, reminding the reader that cruel social criticism in the popular escapist fiction of the time could only rock the boat of convention so far without capsizing it.

In the most frequently anthologized Simon Carne story, "The Duchess of Wiltshire's Diamonds" (first published in the February 1897 issue of *Pearson's Magazine*), Boothby ably demonstrates a talent for literary parody. The author not only caricatures the Sherlock Holmes stories of Sir Arthur Conan Doyle that were so popular with readers in turn-of-the-twentieth-century Britain and America; he satirizes the very form of the amateur detective story itself. In London, Carne adopts the elaborate disguise of the "famous private detective" Klimo, who "has won for himself the right to be considered as great as Lecocq, or even the late lamented Sherlock Holmes." With Klimo, Boothby is obviously responding to the absurdity of the amateur consulting detective, a character who appears uninterested in money, and who works outside of the police, to whom he is vastly superior. Boothby punctuates his parody by stating that Klimo "made his profession pay him well. . . ." Boothby was well aware that no such individual could actually exist in the real world, and that it required a substantial willing suspension of disbelief for the reader to accept a Sherlock Holmes at face value. By having Simon Carne employ his Klimo disguise, Boothby is playfully delineating the unequal contest of intellect and skill between his perceptions of both the amateur consulting detective and the gentleman thief.

The remaining adventures in *A Prince of Swindlers* are equally entertaining. Like all good authors of popular fiction, Boothby's writing style is compelling. The plotting moves along at a brisk pace. The reader is enticed to discover what

Simon Carne's latest spectacular caper will be, every one representing a level of danger that not only threatens to bring Carne to justice, but also (and even more humiliating for a late-Victorian British audience) to expose Carne for a fraud and a cad. Yet Carne has ever the steady hand during his daring exploits, being a master of disguise and trickery, as well as an expert on human nature. High society serves as both his access to wealth and his masquerade. He plans his schemes with bravado, and he never fails. While sailing away from England following Carne's daring theft of the Emperor of Westphalia's expensive gold plate in "An Imperial Finale," his valet, Belton, states, ". . . I must confess I should like to know what they will say when the truth comes out." Carne's reply is both proud and defiant: "I think they'll say that, all things considered, I have won the right to call myself 'A Prince of Swindlers.'"

The spirit of Simon Carne and the gentleman thief has resided within our popular culture in fiction, film, and television for generations. Edward D. Hoch's assortment of Nick Velvet tales—collected in *The Thefts of Nick Velvet* (1978) and *The Velvet Touch* (2000)—offers a perfect example of the gentleman thief's continuing prosperity in popular crime fiction. Noted American crime fiction writer Lawrence Block contributed his own version of the gentleman thief with his Bernie Rhodenbarr novels, which include *Burglars Can't Be Choosers* (1977), *The Burglar in the Closet* (1978), and *The Burglar Who Liked to Quote Kipling* (1979), among others. The Alfred Hitchcock film *To Catch a Thief* (1955) starring Cary Grant as the former cat burglar John Robie (based on the 1952 novel by David Dodge); *The Thomas Crown Affair* (1968), directed by Norman Jewison and starring Steve McQueen as Thomas Crown (remade in 1999 starring Pierce Brosnan); and the popular television series *It Takes a Thief*, starring Robert Wagner and broadcast from 1968 to 1970 on ABC: these are but several of many examples that illustrate the continuing influence and charm of the gentleman thief protagonist. The safecracker Frank (played by James Caan) in director Michael Mann's caper thriller *Thief* (1981) offers a bleak perspective on the gentleman thief protagonist, while director

Blake Edwards's first Inspector Jacques Clouseau film, *The Pink Panther* (1963), presents actor David Niven's Sir Charles Lytton (otherwise known as the notorious thief the Phantom) as a comic figure. A more recent incarnation of the gentleman thief in film is Danny Ocean (played by George Clooney) in director Steven Soderbergh's *Ocean's Eleven* (2001), which was originally released in 1960 starring Frank Sinatra and other members of the famous Hollywood "Rat Pack." Soderbergh's remake was commercially successful enough to inspire two sequels, *Ocean's Twelve* (2004) and *Ocean's Thirteen* (2007).

Why do readers and moviegoers continue to thrill at the exploits of the gentleman thief? Perhaps the answer lies in the fundamentally entertaining and impermissible quality of the story that features a villain as the central character, which also may paradoxically reinforce our appreciation for law, order, and the detection and normalization of the aberrant. Maybe we also enjoy reading about the exploits of fictional devils who delight in breaking morally proscribed social taboos. Conceivably it is because we just admire their panache and charisma. We find ourselves charmed by Simon Carne's suave manner and gentlemanly mannerisms, just as his victims are enchanted. At one point, Lord Amberley says of Carne: "His society was like chloral; the more I took of it the more I wanted." As Mark Twain jokes: "[Go to] heaven for climate, hell for company!" Similarly, as readers of crime fiction, we may appreciate the world inhabited by Sherlock Holmes, but sometimes we simply can't resist the company and con of Simon Carne.

Works Cited

"Boothby, Guy Newell (1867–1905)." *Australian Dictionary of Biography*, Volume 7, 1979. http://adb.anu.edu.au/biography/boothby-guy-newell-5293.

"Death of Guy Boothby." *New York Times*, February 28, 1905. Source: ProQuest Historical Newspapers: *The New York Times* (1851–2009), p. 9.

Depasquale, Paul. *Guy Boothby: His Life and Work*. Seacombe Gardens, Australia: Pioneer Books, 1985.

———. *Guy Boothby: The Science Fiction Connection*. Seacombe Gardens, Australia: Pioneer Books, 1985.

Obituaries Australia. "Boothby, Guy Newell (1867–1905)." From *Advertiser* (Adelaide). http://oa.anu.edu.au/obituary/boothby-guy-newell-5293.

Orwell, George. "Raffles and Miss Blandish." *The Complete Short Stories of Raffles—The Amateur Cracksman* by E. W. Hornung. New York: St. Martin's Press, 1984, 25–38.

A Prince of Swindlers

Preface

BY THE RIGHT HONOURABLE THE EARL OF AMBERLEY,
*for many years Governor of the Colony of New South
Wales, and sometime Viceroy of India*

After no small amount of deliberation, I have come to the conclusion that it is only fit and proper I should set myself right with the world in the matter of the now famous 18— swindles. For, though I have never been openly accused of complicity in those miserable affairs, yet I cannot rid myself of the remembrance that it was I who introduced the man who perpetrated them to London society, and that in more than one instance I acted, innocently enough, Heaven knows, as his *Deus ex machinâ*, in bringing about the very results he was so anxious to achieve. I will first allude, in a few words, to the year in which the crimes took place, and then proceed to describe the events that led to my receiving the confession which has so strangely and unexpectedly come into my hands.

Whatever else may be said on the subject, one thing at least is certain—it will be many years before London forgets that season of festivity. The joyous occasion which made half the sovereigns of Europe our guests for weeks on end, kept foreign princes among us until their faces became as familiar to us as those of our own aristocracy, rendered the houses in our fashionable quarters unobtainable for love or money, filled our hotels to repletion, and produced daily pageants the like of which few of us have ever seen or imagined, can hardly fail to go down to posterity as one of the most notable in English history. Small wonder, therefore, that the wealth, then located in our great metropolis, should have attracted swindlers from all parts of the globe.

That it should have fallen to the lot of one who has always prided himself on steering clear of undesirable acquaintances, to introduce to his friends one of the most notorious adventurers our capital has ever seen, seems like the irony of fate. Perhaps, however, if I begin by showing how cleverly our meeting was contrived, those, who would otherwise feel inclined to censure me, will pause before passing judgment, and will ask themselves whether they would not have walked into the snare as unsuspectingly as I did.

It was during the last year of my term of office as Viceroy, and while I was paying a visit to the Governor of Bombay, that I decided upon making a tour of the northern Provinces, beginning with Peshawur, and winding up with the Maharajah of Malar-Kadir. As the latter potentate is so well known, I need not describe him. His forcible personality, his enlightened rule, and the progress his state has made within the last ten years, are well known to every student of the history of our magnificent Indian Empire.

My stay with him was a pleasant finish to an otherwise monotonous business, for his hospitality has a world-wide reputation. When I arrived he placed his palace, his servants, and his stables at my disposal to use just as I pleased. My time was practically my own. I could be as solitary as a hermit if I so desired; on the other hand, I had but to give the order, and five hundred men would cater for my amusement. It seems therefore the more unfortunate that to this pleasant arrangement I should have to attribute the calamities which it is the purpose of this series of stories to narrate.

On the third morning of my stay I woke early. When I had examined my watch I discovered that it wanted an hour of daylight, and, not feeling inclined to go to sleep again, I wondered how I should employ my time until my servant should bring me my *chota hazri*, or early breakfast. On proceeding to my window I found a perfect morning, the stars still shining, though in the east they were paling before the approach of dawn. It was difficult to realize that in a few hours the earth which now looked so cool and wholesome would be lying, burnt up and quivering, beneath the blazing Indian sun.

I stood and watched the picture presented to me for some minutes, until an overwhelming desire came over me to order a horse and go for a long ride before the sun should make his appearance above the jungle trees. The temptation was more than I could resist, so I crossed the room and, opening the door, woke my servant, who was sleeping in the antechamber. Having bidden him find a groom and have a horse saddled for me, without rousing the household, I returned and commenced my toilet. Then, descending by a private staircase to the great courtyard, I mounted the animal I found awaiting me there, and set off.

Leaving the city behind me I made my way over the new bridge with which His Highness has spanned the river, and, crossing the plain, headed towards the jungle, that rises like a green wall upon the other side. My horse was a *waler* of exceptional excellence, as every one who knows the Maharajah's stable will readily understand, and I was just in the humour for a ride. But the coolness was not destined to last long, for, by the time I had left the second village behind me, the stars had given place to the faint grey light of dawn. A soft breeze stirred the palms and rustled the long grass, but its freshness was deceptive; the sun would be up almost before I could look round, and then nothing could save us from a scorching day.

After I had been riding for nearly an hour it struck me that, if I wished to be back in time for breakfast, I had better think of returning. At the time I was standing in the centre of a small plain, surrounded by jungle. Behind me was the path I had followed to reach the place; in front, and to right and left, others leading whither I could not tell. Having no desire to return by the road I had come, I touched up my horse and cantered off in an easterly direction, feeling certain that, even if I had to make a divergence, I should reach the city without very much trouble.

By the time I had put three miles or so behind me the heat had become stifling, the path being completely shut in on either side by the densest jungle I have ever known. For all I could see to the contrary, I might have been a hundred miles from any habitation.

Imagine my astonishment, therefore, when, on turning a corner of the track, I suddenly left the jungle behind me, and found myself standing on the top of a stupendous cliff, looking down upon a lake of blue water. In the centre of this lake was an island, and on the island a house. At the distance I was from it the latter appeared to be built of white marble, as indeed I afterwards found to be the case. Anything, however, more lovely than the effect produced by the blue water, the white building, and the jungle-clad hills upon the other side, can scarcely be imagined. I stood and gazed at it in delighted amazement. Of all the beautiful places I had hitherto seen in India this, I could honestly say, was entitled to rank first. But how it was to benefit me in my present situation I could not for the life of me understand.

Ten minutes later I had discovered a guide, and also a path down the cliff to the shore, where, I was assured, a boat and a man could be obtained to transport me to the palace. I therefore bade my informant precede me, and after some minutes' anxious scrambling my horse and I reached the water's edge.

Once there, the boatman was soon brought to light, and, when I had resigned my horse to the care of my guide, I was rowed across to the mysterious residence in question.

On reaching it we drew up at some steps leading to a broad stone esplanade, which, I could see, encircled the entire place. Out of a grove of trees rose the building itself, a confused jumble of Eastern architecture crowned with many towers. With the exception of the vegetation and the blue sky, everything was of a dazzling white, against which the dark green of the palms contrasted with admirable effect.

Springing from the boat I made my way up the steps, imbued with much the same feeling of curiosity as the happy Prince, so familiar to us in our nursery days, must have experienced when he found the enchanted castle in the forest. As I reached the top, to my unqualified astonishment, an English man-servant appeared through a gateway and bowed before me.

"Breakfast is served," he said, "and my master bids me say that he waits to receive your lordship."

Though I thought he must be making a mistake, I said nothing, but followed him along the terrace, through a magnificent gateway, on the top of which a peacock was preening himself in the sunlight, through court after court, all built of the same white marble, through a garden in which a fountain was playing to the rustling accompaniment of pipal and pomegranate leaves, to finally enter the verandah of the main building itself.

Drawing aside the curtain which covered a finely-carved doorway, the servant invited me to enter, and as I did so announced "His Excellency the Viceroy."

The change from the vivid whiteness of the marble outside to the cool semi-European room in which I now found myself was almost disconcerting in its abruptness. Indeed, I had scarcely time to recover my presence of mind before I became aware that my host was standing before me. Another surprise was in store for me. I had expected to find a native, instead of which he proved to be an Englishman.

"I am more indebted than I can say to your Excellency for the honour of this visit," he began, as he extended his hand. "I can only wish I were better prepared for it."

"You must not say that," I answered. "It is I who should apologise. I fear I am an intruder. But to tell you the truth I had lost my way, and it is only by chance that I am here at all. I was foolish to venture out without a guide, and have no one to blame for what has occurred but myself."

"In that case I must thank the Fates for their kindness to me," returned my host. "But don't let me keep you standing. You must be both tired and hungry after your long ride, and breakfast, as you see, is upon the table. Shall we show ourselves sufficiently blind to the conventionalities to sit down to it without further preliminaries?"

Upon my assenting he struck a small gong at his side, and servants, acting under the instructions of the white man who had conducted me to his master's presence, instantly appeared in answer to it. We took our places at the table, and the meal immediately commenced.

While it was in progress I was permitted an excellent opportunity of studying my host, who sat opposite me, with such light as penetrated the *jhilmills* falling directly upon his face. I doubt, however, vividly as my memory recalls the scene, whether

I can give you an adequate description of the man who has since come to be a sort of nightmare to me.

In height he could not have been more than five feet two. His shoulders were broad, and would have been evidence of considerable strength but for one malformation, which completely spoilt his whole appearance. The poor fellow suffered from curvature of the spine of the worst sort, and the large hump between his shoulders produced a most extraordinary effect. But it is when I endeavour to describe his face that I find myself confronted with the most serious difficulty.

How to make you realize it I hardly know.

To begin with, I do not think I should be overstepping the mark were I to say that it was one of the most beautiful countenances I have ever seen in my fellow men. Its contour was as perfect as that of the bust of the Greek god, Hermes, to whom, all things considered, it is only fit and proper he should bear some resemblance. The forehead was broad, and surmounted with a wealth of dark hair, in colour almost black. His eyes were large and dreamy, the brows almost pencilled in their delicacy; the nose, the most prominent feature of his face, reminded me more of that of the great Napoleon than any other I can recall.

His mouth was small but firm, his ears as tiny as those of an English beauty, and set in closer to his head than is usual with those organs. But it was his chin that fascinated me most. It was plainly that of a man accustomed to command; that of a man of iron will whom no amount of opposition would deter from his purpose. His hands were small and delicate, and his fingers taper, plainly those of the artist, either a painter or a musician. Altogether he presented a unique appearance, and one that once seen would not be easily forgotten.

During the meal I congratulated him upon the possession of such a beautiful residence, the like of which I had never seen before.

"Unfortunately," he answered, "the place does not belong to me, but is the property of our mutual host, the Maharajah. His Highness, knowing that I am a scholar and a recluse, is kind enough to permit me the use of this portion of the palace; and the value of such a privilege I must leave you to imagine."

"You are a student, then?" I said, as I began to understand matters a little more clearly.

"In a perfunctory sort of way," he replied. "That is to say, I have acquired sufficient knowledge to be aware of my own ignorance."

I ventured to inquire the subject in which he took most interest. It proved to be china and the native art of India, and on these two topics we conversed for upwards of half an hour. It was evident that he was a consummate master of his subject. This I could the more readily understand when, our meal being finished, he led me into an adjoining room, in which stood the cabinets containing his treasures. Such a collection I had never seen before. Its size and completeness amazed me.

"But surely you have not brought all these specimens together yourself?" I asked in astonishment.

"With a few exceptions," he answered. "You see it has been the hobby of my life. And it is to the fact that I am now engaged upon a book upon the subject, which I hope to have published in England next year, that you may attribute my playing the hermit here."

"You intend, then, to visit England?"

"If my book is finished in time," he answered, "I shall be in London at the end of April or the commencement of May. Who would not wish to be in the chief city of Her Majesty's dominions upon such a joyous and auspicious occasion?"

As he said this he took down a small vase from a shelf, and, as if to change the subject, described its history and its beauties to me. A stranger picture than he presented at that moment it would be difficult to imagine. His long fingers held his treasure as carefully as if it were an invaluable jewel, his eyes glistened with the fire of the true collector, who is born but never made, and when he came to that part of his narrative which described the long hunt for, and the eventual purchase of, the ornament in question, his voice fairly shook with excitement. I was more interested than at any other time I should have thought possible, and it was then that I committed the most foolish action of my life. Quite carried away by his charm I said:

"I hope when you *do* come to London, you will permit me to be of any service I can to you."

"I thank you," he answered gravely. "Your lordship is very kind, and if the occasion arises as I hope it will, I shall most certainly avail myself of your offer."

"We shall be very pleased to see you," I replied; "and now, if you will not consider me inquisitive, may I ask if you live in this great place alone?"

"With the exception of my servants I have no companions."

"Really! You must surely find it very lonely?"

"I do, and it is that very solitude which endears it to me. When His Highness so kindly offered me the place for a residence, I inquired if I should have much company. He replied that I might remain here twenty years and never see a soul unless I chose to do so. On hearing that I accepted his offer with alacrity."

"Then you prefer the life of a hermit to mixing with your fellow men?"

"I do. But next year I shall put off my monastic habits for a few months, and mix with my fellow men, as you call them, in London."

"You will find hearty welcome, I am sure."

"It is very kind of you to say so; I hope I shall. But I am forgetting the rules of hospitality. You are a great smoker, I have heard. Let me offer you a cigar."

As he spoke, he took a small silver whistle from his pocket, and blew a peculiar note upon it. A moment later the same English servant who had conducted me to his presence, entered, carrying a number of cigar boxes upon a tray. I chose one, and as I did so glanced at the man. In outward appearance he was exactly what a body servant should be, of medium height, scrupulously neat, clean shaven, and with a face as devoid of expression as a blank wall. When he had left the room again my host immediately turned to me.

"Now," he said, "as you have seen my collection, will you like to explore the Palace?"

To this proposition I gladly assented, and we set off together.

An hour later, satiated with the beauty of what I had seen, and feeling as if I had known the man beside me all my life, I bade him good-bye upon the steps, and prepared to return to the spot where my horse was waiting for me.

"One of my servants will accompany you," he said, "and will conduct you to the city."

"I am greatly indebted to you," I answered. "Should I not see you before, I hope you will not forget your promise to call upon me either in Calcutta, before we leave, or in London next year."

He smiled in a peculiar way.

"You must not think me so blind to my own interests as to forget your kind offer," he replied. "It is just possible, however, that I may be in Calcutta before you leave."

"I shall hope to see you then," I said, and having shaken him by the hand, stepped into the boat which was waiting to convey me across.

Within an hour I was back once more at the Palace, much to the satisfaction of the Maharajah and my staff, to whom my absence had been the cause of considerable anxiety.

It was not until the evening that I found a convenient opportunity, and was able to question His Highness about his strange *protégé*. He quickly told me all there was to know about him. His name, it appeared, was Simon Carne. He was an Englishman, and had been a great traveller. On a certain memorable occasion he had saved His Highness' life at the risk of his own, and ever since that time a close intimacy had existed between them. For upwards of three years the man in question had occupied a wing of the island palace, going away for months at a time, presumably in search of specimens for his collection, and returning when he became tired of the world. To the best of His Highness' belief he was exceedingly wealthy, but on this subject little was known. Such was all I could learn about the mysterious individual I had met earlier in the day.

Much as I wanted to do so, I was unable to pay another visit to the palace on the lake. Owing to pressing business, I was compelled to return to Calcutta as quickly as possible. For this reason it was nearly eight months before I saw or heard anything of Simon Carne again. When I *did* meet him we were in the midst of our preparations for returning to England. I had been for a ride, I remember, and was in the act of dismounting from my horse, when an individual came down the steps and strolled towards me. I recognised him instantly as the man in whom I had been so much interested in Malar-Kadir. He was now dressed in fashionable European attire, but there was no mistaking his face. I held out my hand.

"How do you do, Mr. Carne?" I cried. "This is an unexpected pleasure. Pray how long have you been in Calcutta?"

"I arrived last night," he answered, "and I leave to-morrow morning for Burma. You see, I have taken Your Excellency at your word."

"I am very pleased to see you," I replied. "I have the liveliest recollection of your kindness to me the day that I lost my way in the jungle. As you are leaving so soon, I fear we shall not have the pleasure of seeing much of you, but possibly you can dine with us this evening?"

"I shall be very glad to do so," he answered simply, watching me with his wonderful eyes, which somehow always reminded me of those of a collie.

"Her ladyship is devoted to Indian pottery and brass work," I said, "and she would never forgive me if I did not give her an opportunity of consulting you upon her collection."

"I shall be very proud to assist in any way I can," he answered.

"Very well, then, we shall meet at eight. Good-bye."

That evening we had the pleasure of his society at dinner, and I am prepared to state that a more interesting guest has never sat at a vice-regal table. My wife and daughters fell under his spell as quickly as I had done. Indeed, the former told me afterwards that she considered him the most uncommon man she had met during her residence in the East, an admission scarcely complimentary to the numerous important members of my council who all prided themselves upon their originality. When he said good-bye we had extorted his promise to call upon us in London, and I gathered later that my wife was prepared to make a lion of him when he should put in an appearance.

How he *did* arrive in London during the first week of the following May; how it became known that he had taken Porchester House, which, as every one knows, stands at the corner of Belverton Street and Park Lane, for the season, at an enormous rental; how he furnished it superbly, brought an army of Indian servants to wait upon him, and was prepared to astonish the town with his entertainments, are matters of history. I welcomed him to England, and he dined with us on the night following his arrival, and thus it was that we became, in a manner of speaking, his sponsors in Society. When one looks back on that time, and remembers how vigorously, even in the midst of all that season's gaiety, our social world took him up, the fuss that was made of him, the manner in which his doings were chronicled by the Press, it is indeed hard to realize how egregiously we were all being deceived.

During the months of June and July he was to be met at every house of distinction. Even royalty permitted itself to become on friendly terms with him, while it was rumoured that no fewer than three of the proudest beauties in England were prepared at any moment to accept his offer of marriage. To have been a social lion during such a brilliant season, to have been able to afford one of the most perfect residences in our great city, and to have written a book which the foremost authorities upon the subject declare to be a masterpiece, are things of which any man might be proud. And yet this was exactly what Simon Carne was and did.

And now, having described his advent among us, I must refer to the greatest excitement of all that year. Unique as was the occasion which prompted the gaiety of London, constant as were the arrivals and departures of illustrious folk, marvellous as were the social functions, and enormous the amount of money expended, it is strange that the things which attracted the most attention should be neither royal, social, nor political.

As may be imagined, I am referring to the enormous robberies and swindles which will for ever be associated with that memorable year. Day after day, for weeks at a time, the Press chronicled a series of crimes, the like of which the oldest Englishman could not remember. It soon became evident that they were the work of one person, and that that person was a master hand was as certain as his success.

At first the police were positive that the depredations were conducted by a foreign gang, located somewhere in North London, and that they would soon be able to put their fingers on the culprits. But they were speedily undeceived. In spite of their efforts the burglaries continued with painful regularity. Hardly a prominent person escaped. My friend Lord Orpington was despoiled of his priceless gold and silver plate; my cousin, the Duchess of Wiltshire, lost her world famous diamonds; the Earl of Calingforth his racehorse "Vulcanite"; and others of my friends were despoiled of their choicest possessions. How it was that I escaped I can understand now, but I must confess that it passed my comprehension at the time.

Throughout the season Simon Carne and I scarcely spent a day apart. His society was like chloral; the more I took of it the more I wanted. And I am now told that others were affected in the same way. I used to flatter myself that it was to my endeavours he owed his social success, and I can only, in justice, say that he tried to prove himself grateful. I have his portrait hanging in my library now, painted by a famous Academician, with this inscription upon the lozenge at the base of the frame:

"To my kind friend, the Earl of Amberley, in remembrance of a happy and prosperous visit to London, from Simon Carne."

The portrait represents him standing before a bookcase in a half-dark room. His extraordinary face, with its dark penetrating eyes, is instinct with life, while his lips seem as if opening to speak. To my thinking it would have been a better picture had he not been standing in such a way that the light accentuated his deformity; but it appears that this was the sitter's own desire, thus confirming what, on many occasions, I had felt compelled to believe, namely, that he was, for some peculiar reason, proud of his misfortune.

It was at the end of the Cowes week that we parted company. He had been racing his yacht, the *Unknown Quantity*, and, as if not satisfied with having won the Derby, must needs appropriate the Queen's Cup. It was on the day following that now famous race that half the leaders of London Society bade him farewell on the deck of the steam yacht that was to carry him back to India.

A month later, and quite by chance, the dreadful truth came out. Then it was discovered that the man of whom we had all been making so much fuss, the man whom royalty had condescended to treat almost as a friend, was neither more nor less than a Prince of Swindlers, who had been utilising his splendid opportunities to the very best advantage.

Every one will remember the excitement which followed the first disclosure of this dreadful secret, and the others which followed it. As fresh discoveries came to light, the popular interest became more and more intense, while the public's wonderment at the man's almost superhuman cleverness waxed every day greater than before. My position, as you may suppose, was not an enviable one. I saw how cleverly I had been duped, and when my friends, who had most of them suffered from his talents, congratulated me on my immunity, I could only console myself with the reflection that I was responsible for more than half the acquaintances the wretch had made. But, deeply as I was drinking of the cup of sorrow, I had not come to the bottom of it yet.

One Saturday evening—the 7th of November, if I recollect aright—I was sitting in my library, writing letters after dinner, when I heard the postman come round the square and finally ascend the steps of my house. A few moments later a footman entered bearing some letters, and a large packet, upon a salver. Having read the former, I cut the string which bound the parcel, and opened it.

To my surprise, it contained a bundle of manuscript and a letter. The former I put aside, while I broke open the envelope and extracted its contents. To my horror, it was from Simon Carne, and ran as follows:

On the High Seas.

My Dear Lord Amberley,—

"It is only reasonable to suppose that by this time you have become acquainted with the nature of the peculiar services you have rendered me. I am your debtor for as pleasant, and, at the same time, as profitable a visit to London as any man could desire. In order that you may not think me ungrateful, I will ask you to accept the accompanying narrative of my adventures in your great metropolis. Since I have placed myself beyond the reach of capture, I will permit you to make any use of it you please. Doubtless you will blame me, but you must at least do me the justice to remember that, in spite of the splendid opportunities you permitted me, I invariably spared yourself and family. You will think me mad thus to betray myself, but, believe me, I have taken the greatest precautions against discovery, and as I am proud of my London exploits, I have not the least desire to hide my light beneath a bushel.

With kind regards to Lady Amberley and yourself,

I am, yours very sincerely,
Simon Carne.

Needless to say I did not retire to rest before I had read the manuscript through from beginning to end, with the result that the morning following I communicated with the police. They were hopeful that they might be able to discover the place where the packet had been posted, but after considerable search it was found that it had been handed by a captain of a yacht, name unknown, to the commander of a homeward bound brig, off Finisterre, for postage in Plymouth. The narrative, as you will observe, is written in the third person, and, as far as I can gather, the handwriting is not that of Simon Carne. As, however, the details of each individual swindle coincide exactly with the facts as ascertained by the police, there can be no doubt of their authenticity.

A year has now elapsed since my receipt of the packet.

During that time the police of almost every civilized country have been on the alert to effect the capture of my whilom friend, but without success. Whether his yacht sank and conveyed him to the bottom of the ocean, or whether, as I suspect, she only carried him to a certain part of the seas where he changed into another vessel and so eluded justice, I cannot say. Even the Maharajah of Malar-Kadir has heard nothing of him since. The fact, however, remains, I have, innocently enough, compounded a series of felonies, and, as I said at the commencement of this preface, the publication of the narrative I have so strangely received is intended to be, as far as possible, my excuse.

Introduction

The night was close and muggy, such a night, indeed, as only Calcutta, of all the great cities of the East, can produce. The reek of the native quarter, that sickly, penetrating odour which, once smelt, is never forgotten, filled the streets and even invaded the sacred precincts of Government House, where a man of gentlemanly appearance, but sadly deformed, was engaged in bidding Her Majesty the Queen of England's representative in India an almost affectionate farewell.

"You will not forget your promise to acquaint us with your arrival in London," said His Excellency as he shook his guest by the hand. "We shall be delighted to see you, and if we can make your stay pleasurable as well as profitable to you, you may be sure we shall endeavour to do so."

"Your lordship is most hospitable, and I think I may safely promise that I will avail myself of your kindness," replied the other. "In the meantime 'good-bye,' and a pleasant voyage to you."

A few minutes later he had passed the sentry, and was making his way along the Maidan to the point where the Chitpore Road crosses it. Here he stopped and appeared to deliberate. He smiled a little sardonically as the recollection of the evening's entertainment crossed his mind, and, as if he feared he might forget something connected with it, when he reached a lamp-post, took a note-book from his pocket and made an entry in it.

"Providence has really been most kind," he said as he shut the book with a snap, and returned it to his pocket. "And what is more, I am prepared to be properly grateful. It was a good morning's work for me when His Excellency decided to take a ride through the Maharajah's suburbs. Now I have only to play my cards carefully and success should be assured."

He took a cigar from his pocket, nipped off the end, and then lit it. He was still smiling when the smoke had cleared away.

"It is fortunate that Her Excellency is, like myself, an enthusiastic admirer of Indian art," he said. "It is a trump card, and I shall play it for all it's worth when I get to the other side. But to-night I have something of more importance to consider. I have to find the sinews of war. Let us hope that the luck which has followed me hitherto will still hold good, and that Liz will prove as tractable as usual."

Almost as he concluded his soliloquy a *ticcagharri* made its appearance, and, without being hailed, pulled up beside him. It was evident that their meeting was intentional, for the driver asked no question of his fare, who simply took his seat, laid himself back upon the cushions, and smoked his cigar with the air of a man playing a part in some performance that had been long arranged.

Ten minutes later the coachman had turned out of the Chitpore Road into a narrow bye street. From this he broke off into another, and at the end of a few minutes into still another. These offshoots of the main thoroughfare were wrapped in inky darkness, and, in order that there should be as much danger as possible, they were crowded to excess. To those who know Calcutta this information will be significant.

There are slums in all the great cities of the world, and every one boasts its own peculiar characteristics. The Ratcliffe Highway in London, and the streets that lead off it, can show a fair assortment of vice; the Chinese quarters of New York, Chicago, and San Francisco can more than equal them; Little Bourke Street, Melbourne, a portion of Singapore, and the shipping quarter of Bombay, have their own individual qualities, but surely for the lowest of all the world's low places one must go to Calcutta, the capital of our great Indian Empire.

Surrounding the Lal, Machua, Burra, and Joira Bazaars are to be found the most infamous dens the mind of man can conceive. But that is not all. If an exhibition of scented, high-toned, gold-lacquered vice is required, one has only to make one's way into the streets that lie within a stone's throw of the Chitpore Road to be accommodated.

Reaching a certain corner, the *gharri* came to a standstill and the fare alighted. He said something in an undertone to the driver as he paid him, and then stood upon the footway placidly smoking until the vehicle had disappeared from view. When it was no longer in sight he looked up at the houses towering above his head; in one a marriage feast was being celebrated; across the way the sound of a woman's voice in angry expostulation could be heard. The passers-by, all of whom were natives, scanned him curiously, but made no remark. Englishmen, it is true, were *sometimes* seen in that quarter and at that hour, but this one seemed of a different class, and it is possible that nine out of every ten took him for the most detested of all Englishmen, a police officer.

For upwards of ten minutes he waited, but after that he seemed to become impatient. The person he had expected to find at the rendezvous had, so far, failed to put in an appearance, and he was beginning to wonder what he had better do in the event of his not coming.

But, badly as he had started, he was not destined to fail in his enterprise; for, just as his patience was exhausted, he saw, hastening towards him, a man whom he recognised as the person for whom he waited.

"You are late," he said in English, which he was aware the other spoke fluently, though he was averse to owning it. "I have been here more than a quarter of an hour."

"It was impossible that I could get away before," the other answered cringingly; "but if your Excellency will be pleased to follow me now, I will conduct you to the person you seek, without further delay."

"Lead on," said the Englishman; "we have wasted enough time already."

Without more ado the Babu turned himself about and proceeded in the direction he had come, never pausing save to glance over his shoulder to make sure that his companion was following. Seemingly countless were the lanes, streets, and alleys through which they passed. The place was nothing more or less than a rabbit warren of small passages, and so dark that, at times, it was as much as the Englishman could do to see his guide ahead of him. Well acquainted as he was with the quarter, he had never been able to make himself master of all its intricacies, and as the person whom he was going to meet was compelled to change her residence at frequent intervals, he had long given up the idea of endeavouring to find her himself.

Turning out of a narrow lane, which differed from its fellows only in the fact that it contained more dirt and a greater number of unsavoury odours, they found themselves at the top of a short flight of steps, which in their turn conducted them to a small square, round which rose houses taller than any they had yet discovered. Every window contained a balcony, some larger than others, but all in the last stage of decay. The effect was peculiar, but not so strange as the quiet of the place; indeed, the wind and the far off hum of the city were the only sounds to be heard.

Now and again figures issued from the different doorways, stood for a moment looking anxiously about them, and then disappeared as silently as they had come. All the time not a light was to be seen, or the sound of a human voice. It was a strange place for a white man to be in, and so Simon Carne evidently thought as he obeyed his guide's invitation and entered the last house on the right hand side.

Whether the buildings had been originally intended for residences or for offices it would be difficult to say. They were almost as old as John Company himself, and would not appear to have been cleaned or repaired since they had been first inhabited.

From the centre of the hall, in which he found himself, a massive staircase led to the other floors, and up this Carne marched behind his conductor. On gaining the first landing he paused while the Babu went forward and knocked at a door. A moment later the shutter of a small *grille* was pulled back, and the face of a native woman looked out. A muttered conversation ensued, and after it was finished the door was opened and

Carne was invited to enter. This summons he obeyed with alacrity, only to find that once he was inside, the door was immediately shut and barred behind him.

After the darkness of the street and the semi-obscurity of the stairs, the dazzling light of the apartment in which he now stood was almost too much for his eyes. It was not long, however, before he had recovered sufficiently to look about him. The room was a fine one, in shape almost square, with a large window at the further end covered with a thick curtain of native cloth. It was furnished with considerable taste, in a mixture of styles, half European and half native. A large lamp of worked brass, burning some sweet-smelling oil, was suspended from the ceiling. A quantity of tapestry, much of it extremely rare, covered the walls, relieved here and there with some superb specimens of native weapons; comfortable divans were scattered about, as if inviting repose, and as if further to carry out this idea, beside one of the lounges, a silver-mounted narghyle was placed, its tube curled up beside it in a fashion somewhat suggestive of a snake.

But, luxurious as it all was, it was evidently not quite what Carne had expected to find, and the change seemed to mystify as much as it surprised him. Just as he was coming to a decision, however, his ear caught the sound of chinking bracelets, and next moment the curtain which covered a doorway in the left wall was drawn aside by a hand glistening with rings and as tiny as that of a little child. A second later Trincomalee Liz entered the room.

Standing in the doorway, the heavily embroidered curtain falling in thick folds behind her and forming a most effective background, she made a picture such as few men could look upon without a thrill of admiration. At that time she, the famous Trincomalee Liz, whose doings had made her notorious from the Saghalian coast to the shores of the Persian Gulf, was at the prime of her life and beauty—a beauty such as no man who has ever seen it will ever forget.

It was a notorious fact that those tiny hands had ruined more men than any other half-dozen pairs in the whole of India, or the East for that matter. Not much was known of her history, but what had come to light was certainly interesting. As far as could be ascertained she was born in Tonquin; her father, it had been said, was a handsome but disreputable Frenchman, who had called himself a count, and over his absinthe was wont to talk of his possessions in Normandy; her mother hailed from Northern India, and she herself was lovelier than the pale hibiscus blossom. To tell in what manner Liz and Carne had become acquainted would be too long a story to be included here. But that there *was* some bond between the pair is a fact that may be stated without fear of contradiction.

On seeing her, the visitor rose from his seat and went to meet her.

"So you have come at last," she said, holding out both hands to him. "I have been expecting you these three weeks past. Remember, you told me you were coming."

"I was prevented," said Carne. "And the business upon which I desired to see you was not fully matured."

"So there is business then?" she answered with a pretty petulance. "I thought as much. I might know by this time that you do not come to see me for anything else. But there, do not let us talk in this fashion when I have not had you with me for nearly a year. Tell me of yourself, and what you have been doing since last we met."

As she spoke she was occupied preparing a *huqa* for him. When it was ready she fitted a tiny amber mouthpiece to the tube, and presented it to him with a compliment as delicate as her own rose-leaf hands. Then, seating herself on a pile of cushions beside him, she bade him proceed with his narrative.

"And now," she said, when he had finished, "what is this business that brings you to me?"

A few moments elapsed before he began his explanation, and during that time he studied her face closely.

"I have a scheme in my head," he said, laying the *huqa* stick carefully upon the floor, "that, properly carried out, should make us both rich beyond all telling, but to carry it out properly I must have your co-operation."

She laughed softly, and nodded her head.

"You mean that you want money," she answered. "Ah, Simon, you always want money."

"I *do* want money," he replied without hesitation. "I want it badly. Listen to what I have to say, and then tell me if you can give it to me. You know what year this is in England?"

She nodded her head. There were few things with which she had not some sort of acquaintance.

"It will be a time of great rejoicing," he continued. "Half the princes of the earth will be assembled in London. There will be wealth untold there, to be had for the mere gathering in; and who is so well able to gather it as I? I tell you, Liz, I have made up my mind to make the journey and try my luck, and, if you will help me with the money, you shall have it back with such jewels, for interest, as no woman ever wore yet. To begin with, there is the Duchess of Wiltshire's necklace. Ah, your eyes light up; you have heard of it?"

"I have," she answered, her voice trembling with excitement. "Who has not?"

"It is the finest thing of its kind in Europe, if not in the world," he went on slowly, as if to allow time for his words to sink in. "It consists of three hundred stones, and is worth, apart from its historic value, at least fifty thousand pounds."

He saw her hands tighten on the cushions upon which she sat.

"Fifty thousand pounds! That is five lacs of rupees?"

"Exactly! Five lacs of rupees, a king's ransom," he answered. "But that is not all. There will be twice as much to be had for the taking when once I get there. Find me the money I want, and those stones shall be your property."

"How much *do* you want?"

"The value of the necklace," he answered. "Fifty thousand pounds."

"It is a large sum," she said, "and it will be difficult to find."

He smiled, as if her words were a joke and should be treated as such.

"The interest will be good," he answered.

"But are you certain of obtaining it?" she asked.

"Have I ever failed yet?" he replied.

"You have done wonderful things, certainly. But this time you are attempting so much."

"The greater the glory!" he answered. "I have prepared my plans, and I shall not fail. This is going to be the greatest undertaking of my life. If it comes off successfully, I shall retire upon my laurels. Come, for the sake of—well, you know for the sake of what—will you let me have the money? It is not the first time you have done it, and on each occasion you have not only been repaid, but well rewarded into the bargain."

"When do you want it?"

"By mid-day to-morrow. It must be paid in to my account at the Bank before twelve o'clock. You will have no difficulty in obtaining it I know. Your respectable merchant friends will do it for you if you but hold up your little finger. If they don't feel inclined, then put on the screw and make them."

She laughed as he paid this tribute to her power. A moment later, however, she was all gravity.

"And the security?"

He leant towards her and whispered in her ear.

"It is well," she replied. "The money shall be found for you to-morrow. Now tell me your plans; I must know all that you intend doing."

"In the first place," he answered, drawing a little closer to her, and speaking in a lower voice, so that no eavesdropper should hear, "I shall take with me Abdul Khan, Ram Gafur, Jowur Singh, and Nur Ali, with others of less note as servants. I shall engage the best house in London, and under the wing of our gracious Viceroy, who has promised me the light of his countenance, will work my way into the highest society. That done I shall commence operations. No one will ever suspect!"

"And when it is finished, and you have accomplished your desires, how will you escape?"

"That I have not yet arranged. But of this you may be sure, I shall run no risks."

"And afterwards?"

He leant a little towards her again, and patted her affectionately upon the hand.

"Then we shall see what we shall see," he said. "I don't think you will find me ungrateful."

She shook her pretty head.

"It is good talk," she cried, "but it means nothing. You always say the same. How am I to know that you will not learn to love one of the white mem-sahibs when you are so much among them?"

"Because there is but one Trincomalee Liz," he answered; "and for that reason you need have no fear."

Her face expressed the doubt with which she received this assertion. As she had said, it was not the first time she had been cajoled into advancing him large sums with the same assurance. He knew this, and, lest she should alter her mind, prepared to change the subject.

"Besides the others, I must take Hiram Singh and Wajib Baksh. They are in Calcutta, I am told, and I must communicate with them before noon to-morrow. They are the most expert craftsmen in India, and I shall have need of them."

"I will have them found, and word shall be sent to you."

"Could I not meet them here?"

"Nay, it is impossible. I shall not be here myself. I leave for Madras within six hours."

"Is there, then, trouble toward?"

She smiled, and spread her hands apart with a gesture that said: "Who knows?"

He did not question her further, but after a little conversation on the subject of the money, rose to bid her farewell.

"I do not like this idea," she said, standing before him and looking him in the face. "It is too dangerous. Why should you run such risk? Let us go together to Burma. You shall be my vizier."

"I would wish for nothing better," he said, "were it not that I am resolved to go to England. My mind is set upon it, and when I have done, London shall have something to talk about for years to come."

"If you are determined, I will say no more," she answered; "but when it is over, and you are free, we will talk again."

"You will not forget about the money?" he asked anxiously. She stamped her foot.

"Money, money, money," she cried. "It is always the money of which you think. But you shall have it, never fear. And now when shall I see you again?"

"In six months' time at a place of which I will tell you beforehand."

"It is a long time to wait."

"There is a necklace worth five lacs to pay you for the waiting."

"Then I will be patient. Good-bye."

"Good-bye, little friend," he said. And then, as if he thought he had not said enough, he added: "Think sometimes of Simon Carne."

She promised, with many pretty speeches, to do so, after which he left the room and went downstairs. As he reached the bottom step he heard a cough in the dark above him and looked up. He could just distinguish Liz leaning over the rail. Then something dropped and rattled upon the wooden steps behind him. He picked it up to find that it was an antique ring set with rubies.

"Wear it that it may bring thee luck," she cried, and then disappeared again.

He put the present on his finger and went out into the dark square.

"The money is found," he said, as he looked up at the starlit heavens. "Hiram Singh and Wajib Baksh are to be discovered before noon to-morrow. His Excellency the Viceroy and his amiable lady have promised to stand sponsors for me in London society. If with these advantages I don't succeed, well, all I can say is, I don't deserve to. Now where is my Babuji?"

Almost at the same instant a figure appeared from the shadow of the building and approached him.

"If the Sahib will permit me, I will guide him by a short road to his hotel."

"Lead on then. I am tired, and it is time I was in bed." Then to himself he added: "I must sleep to-night, for to-morrow there are great things toward."

CHAPTER I

THE DUCHESS OF
WILTSHIRE'S DIAMONDS

To the reflective mind the rapidity with which the inhabitants of the world's greatest city seize upon a new name or idea, and familiarise themselves with it, can scarcely prove otherwise than astonishing. As an illustration of my meaning let me take the case of Klimo—the now famous private detective, who has won for himself the right to be considered as great as Lecocq, or even the late lamented Sherlock Holmes.

Up to a certain morning London had never even heard his name, nor had it the remotest notion as to who or what he might be. It was as sublimely ignorant and careless on the subject as the inhabitants of Kamtchatka or Peru. Within twenty-four hours, however, the whole aspect of the case was changed. The man, woman, or child who had not seen his posters, or heard his name, was counted an ignoramus unworthy of intercourse with human beings.

Princes became familiar with it as their trains bore them to Windsor to luncheon with the Queen; the nobility noticed and commented upon it as they drove about the town; merchants, and business men generally, read it as they made their ways by omnibus or underground, to their various shops and counting-houses; street boys called each other by it as a nickname; music hall artistes introduced it into their patter, while it was even rumoured that the Stock Exchange itself had paused in the full flood tide of business to manufacture a riddle on the subject.

That Klimo made his profession pay him well was certain, first from the fact that his advertisements must have cost a good round sum, and, second, because he had taken a mansion in Belverton Street, Park Lane, next door to Porchester House, where, to the dismay of that aristocratic neighbourhood, he advertised that he was prepared to receive and be consulted by his clients. The invitation was responded to with alacrity, and from that day forward, between the hours of twelve and two, the pavement upon the north side of the street was lined with carriages, every one containing some person desirous of testing the great man's skill.

I must here explain that I have narrated all this in order to show the state of affairs existing in Belverton Street and Park Lane when Simon Carne arrived, or was supposed to arrive, in England. If my memory serves me correctly, it was on Wednesday, the 3rd of May, that the Earl of Amberley drove to Victoria to meet and welcome the man whose acquaintance he had made in India under such peculiar circumstances, and under the spell of whose fascination he and his family had fallen so completely.

Reaching the station, his lordship descended from his carriage, and made his way to the platform set apart for the reception of the Continental express. He walked with a jaunty air, and seemed to be on the best of terms with himself and the world in general. How little he suspected the existence of the noose into which he was so innocently running his head!

As if out of compliment to his arrival, the train put in an appearance within a few moments of his reaching the platform. He immediately placed himself in such a position that he could make sure of seeing the man he wanted, and waited patiently until he should come in sight. Carne, however, was not among the first batch; indeed, the majority of passengers had passed before his lordship caught sight of him.

One thing was very certain, however great the crush might have been, it would have been difficult to mistake Carne's figure. The man's infirmity and the peculiar beauty of his face rendered him easily recognisable. Possibly, after his long sojourn in India, he found the morning cold, for he wore a long fur coat, the collar of which he had turned up round his ears, thus making a fitting frame for his delicate face. On seeing Lord Amberley he hastened forward to greet him.

"This is most kind and friendly of you," he said, as he shook the other by the hand. "A fine day and Lord Amberley to meet me. One could scarcely imagine a better welcome."

As he spoke, one of his Indian servants approached and salaamed before him. He gave him an order, and received an answer in Hindustani, whereupon he turned again to Lord Amberley.

"You may imagine how anxious I am to see my new dwelling," he said. "My servant tells me that my carriage is here, so may I hope that you will drive back with me and see for yourself how I am likely to be lodged?"

"I shall be delighted," said Lord Amberley, who was longing for the opportunity, and they accordingly went out into the station yard together to discover a brougham, drawn by two magnificent horses, and with Nur Ali, in all the glory of white raiment and crested turban, on the box, waiting to receive them. His lordship dismissed his Victoria, and when Jowur Singh had taken his place beside his fellow servant upon the box, the carriage rolled out of the station yard in the direction of Hyde Park.

"I trust her ladyship is quite well," said Simon Carne politely, as they turned into Gloucester Place.

"Excellently well, thank you," replied his lordship. "She bade me welcome you to England in her name as well as my own, and I was to say that she is looking forward to seeing you."

"She is most kind, and I shall do myself the honour of calling upon her as soon as circumstances will permit," answered Carne. "I beg you will convey my best thanks to her for her thought of me."

While these polite speeches were passing between them they were rapidly approaching a large hoarding, on which was displayed a poster setting forth the name of the now famous detective, Klimo.

Simon Carne, leaning forward, studied it, and when they had passed, turned to his friend again.

"At Victoria and on all the hoardings we meet I see an enormous placard, bearing the word 'Klimo.' Pray, what does it mean?"

His lordship laughed.

"You are asking a question which, a month ago, was on the lips of nine out of every ten Londoners. It is only within the last fortnight that we have learned who and what 'Klimo' is."

"And pray what is he?"

"Well, the explanation is very simple. He is neither more nor less than a remarkably astute private detective, who has succeeded in attracting notice in such a way that half London has been induced to patronize him. I have had no dealings with the man myself. But a friend of mine, Lord Orpington, has been the victim of a most audacious burglary, and, the police having failed to solve the mystery, he has called Klimo in. We shall therefore see what he can do before many days are past. But, there, I expect you will soon know more about him than any of us."

"Indeed! And why?"

"For the simple reason that he has taken No. 1, Belverton Terrace, the house adjoining your own, and sees his clients there."

Simon Carne pursed up his lips, and appeared to be considering something.

"I trust he will not prove a nuisance," he said at last. "The agents who found me the house should have acquainted me with the fact. Private detectives, on however large a scale, scarcely strike one as the most desirable of neighbours—particularly for a man who is so fond of quiet as myself."

At this moment they were approaching their destination. As the carriage passed Belverton Street and pulled up, Lord Amberley pointed to a long line of vehicles standing before the detective's door.

"You can see for yourself something of the business he does," he said. "Those are the carriages of his clients, and it is probable that twice as many have arrived on foot."

"I shall certainly speak to the agent on the subject," said Carne, with a shadow of annoyance upon his face. "I consider the fact of this man's being so close to me a serious drawback to the house."

Jowur Singh here descended from the box and opened the

door in order that his master and his guest might alight, while portly Ram Gafur, the butler, came down the steps and salaamed before them with Oriental obsequiousness. Carne greeted his domestics with kindly condescension, and then, accompanied by the ex-Viceroy, entered his new abode.

"I think you may congratulate yourself upon having secured one of the most desirable residences in London," said his lordship ten minutes or so later, when they had explored the principal rooms.

"I am very glad to hear you say so," said Carne. "I trust your lordship will remember that you will always be welcome in the house as long as I am its owner."

"It is very kind of you to say so," returned Lord Amberley warmly. "I shall look forward to some months of pleasant intercourse. And now I must be going. To-morrow, perhaps, if you have nothing better to do, you will give us the pleasure of your company at dinner. Your fame has already gone abroad, and we shall ask one or two nice people to meet you, including my brother and sister-in-law, Lord and Lady Gelpington, Lord and Lady Orpington, and my cousin, the Duchess of Wiltshire, whose interest in china and Indian art, as perhaps you know, is only second to your own."

"I shall be most glad to come."

"We may count on seeing you in Eaton Square, then, at eight o'clock?"

"If I am alive you may be sure I shall be there. Must you really go? Then good-bye and many thanks for meeting me."

His lordship having left the house, Simon Carne went upstairs to his dressing-room, which it was to be noticed he found without inquiry, and rang the electric bell, beside the fireplace, three times. While he was waiting for it to be answered he stood looking out of the window at the long line of carriages in the street below.

"Everything is progressing admirably," he said to himself. "Amberley does not suspect any more than the world in general. As a proof he asks me to dinner to-morrow evening to meet his brother and sister-in-law, two of his particular friends, and above all Her Grace of Wiltshire. Of course I shall go, and when I bid Her Grace good-bye it will be strange if I am not one step nearer the interest on Liz's money."

At this moment the door opened, and his valet, the grave and respectable Belton, entered the room. Carne turned to greet him impatiently.

"Come, come, Belton," he said, "we must be quick. It is twenty minutes to twelve, and if we don't hurry, the folk next door will become impatient. Have you succeeded in doing what I spoke to you about last night?"

"I have done everything, sir."

"I am glad to hear it. Now lock that door and let us get to work. You can let me have your news while I am dressing."

Opening one side of a massive wardrobe, that completely filled one end of the room, Belton took from it a number of garments. They included a well-worn velvet coat, a baggy pair of trousers—so old that only a notorious pauper or a million-aire could have afforded to wear them—a flannel waistcoat, a Gladstone collar, a soft silk tie, and a pair of embroidered car-pet slippers upon which no old clothes man in the most reck-less way of business in Petticoat Lane would have advanced a single halfpenny. Into these he assisted his master to change.

"Now give me the wig, and unfasten the straps of this hump," said Carne, as the other placed the garments just referred to upon a neighbouring chair.

Belton did as he was ordered, and then there happened a thing the like of which no one would have believed. Having unbuckled a strap on either shoulder, and slipped his hand beneath the waistcoat, he withdrew a large *papier-maché* hump, which he carried away and carefully placed in a drawer of the bureau. Relieved of his burden, Simon Carne stood up as straight and well-made a man as any in Her Majesty's dominions. The malformation, for which so many, including the Earl and Countess of Amberley, had often pitied him, was nothing but a hoax intended to produce an effect which would permit him additional facilities of disguise.

The hump discarded, and the grey wig fitted carefully to his head in such a manner that not even a pinch of his own curly locks could be seen beneath it, he adorned his cheeks with a pair of *crépu*-hair whiskers, donned the flannel vest and the velvet coat previously mentioned, slipped his feet into the carpet slippers, placed a pair of smoked glasses upon his nose, and declared himself ready to proceed about his business. The man who would have known him for Simon Carne would have been as astute as, well, shall we say, as the private detective—Klimo himself.

"It's on the stroke of twelve," he said, as he gave a final glance at himself in the pier-glass above the dressing-table, and arranged his tie to his satisfaction. "Should any one call, instruct Ram Gafur to tell them that I have gone out on business, and shall not be back until three o'clock."

"Very good, sir."

"Now undo the door and let me go in."

Thus commanded, Belton went across to the large wardrobe which, as I have already said, covered the whole of one side of the room, and opened the middle door. Two or three garments were seen inside suspended on pegs, and these he removed, at the same time pushing towards the right the panel at the rear. When this was done a large aperture in the wall between the two houses was disclosed. Through this door Carne passed, drawing it behind him.

In No. 1, Belverton Terrace, the house occupied by the detective, whose presence in the street Carne seemed to find so objectionable, the entrance thus constructed was covered by the peculiar kind of confessional box in which Klimo invariably sat to receive his clients, the rearmost panels of which opened in the same fashion as those in the wardrobe in the dressing-room. These being pulled aside, he had but to draw them to again after him, take his seat, ring the electric bell to inform his housekeeper that he was ready, and then welcome his clients as quickly as they cared to come.

Punctually at two o'clock the interviews ceased, and Klimo, having reaped an excellent harvest of fees, returned to Porchester House to become Simon Carne once more.

Possibly it was due to the fact that the Earl and Countess of Amberley were brimming over with his praise, or it may have been the rumour that he was worth as many millions as you have fingers upon your hand that did it; one thing, however, was self evident, within twenty-four hours of the noble earl's meeting him at Victoria Station, Simon Carne was the talk, not only of fashionable, but also of unfashionable London.

That his household were, with one exception, natives of India, that he had paid a rental for Porchester House which ran into five figures, that he was the greatest living authority upon china and Indian art generally, and that he had come over to England in search of a wife, were among the smallest of the *canards* set afloat concerning him.

During dinner next evening Carne put forth every effort to please. He was placed on the right hand of his hostess and next to the Duchess of Wiltshire. To the latter he paid particular attention, and to such good purpose that when the ladies returned to the drawing-room afterwards, Her Grace was full of his praises. They had discussed china of all sorts, Carne had promised her a specimen which she had longed for all her life, but had never been able to obtain, and in return she had promised to show him the quaintly carved Indian casket in which the famous necklace, of which he had, of course, heard, spent most of its time. She would be wearing the jewels in question at her own ball in a week's time, she informed him, and if he would care to see the case when it came from her bankers on that day, she would be only too pleased to show it to him.

As Simon Carne drove home in his luxurious brougham afterwards, he smiled to himself as he thought of the success which was attending his first endeavour. Two of the guests, who were stewards of the Jockey Club, had heard with delight his idea of purchasing a horse, in order to have an interest in the Derby. While another, on hearing that he desired to become the possessor of a yacht, had offered to propose him for the R.C.Y.C. To crown it all, however, and much better than all, the Duchess of Wiltshire had promised to show him her famous diamonds.

"By this time next week," he said to himself, "Liz's interest should be considerably closer. But satisfactory as my progress has been hitherto, it is difficult to see how I am to get possession of the stones. From what I have been able to discover, they are only brought from the bank on the day the Duchess intends to wear them, and they are taken back by His Grace the morning following.

"While she has got them on her person it would be manifestly impossible to get them from her. And as, when she takes them off, they are returned to their box and placed in a safe, constructed in the wall of the bedroom adjoining, and which for the occasion is occupied by the butler and one of the under footmen, the only key being in the possession of the Duke himself, it would be equally foolish to hope to appropriate them. In what manner, therefore, I am to become their possessor passes my comprehension. However, one thing is certain, obtained they must be, and the attempt must be made on the night of the ball if possible. In the meantime I'll set my wits to work upon a plan."

Next day Simon Carne was the recipient of an invitation to the ball in question, and two days later he called upon the Duchess of Wiltshire, at her residence in Belgrave Square, with a plan prepared. He also took with him the small vase he had promised her four nights before. She received him most graciously, and their talk fell at once into the usual channel. Having examined her collection, and charmed her by means of one or two judicious criticisms, he asked permission to include photographs of certain of her treasures in his forthcoming book, then little by little he skilfully guided the conversation on to the subject of jewels.

"Since we are discussing gems, Mr. Carne," she said, "perhaps it would interest you to see my famous necklace. By good fortune I have it in the house now, for the reason that an alteration is being made to one of the clasps by my jewellers."

"I should like to see it immensely," answered Carne. "At one time and another I have had the good fortune to examine the jewels of the leading Indian princes, and I should like to be able to say that I had seen the famous Wiltshire necklace."

"Then you shall certainly have that honour," she answered with a smile. "If you will ring that bell I will send for it."

Carne rang the bell as requested, and when the butler entered he was given the key of the safe and ordered to bring the case to the drawing-room.

"We must not keep it very long," she observed while the man was absent. "It is to be returned to the bank in an hour's time."

"I am indeed fortunate," Carne replied, and turned to the description of some curious Indian wood carving, of which he was making a special feature in his book. As he explained, he had collected his illustrations from the doors of Indian temples, from the gateways of palaces, from old brass work, and even from carved chairs and boxes he had picked up in all sorts of odd corners. Her Grace was most interested.

"How strange that you should have mentioned it," she said. "If carved boxes have any interest for you, it is possible my jewel case itself may be of use to you. As I think I told you during Lady Amberley's dinner, it came from Benares, and has carved upon it the portraits of nearly every god in the Hindu Pantheon."

"You raise my curiosity to fever heat," said Carne.

A few moments later the servant returned, bringing with him a wooden box, about sixteen inches long, by twelve wide, and eight deep, which he placed upon a table beside his mistress, after which he retired.

"This is the case to which I have just been referring," said the Duchess, placing her hand on the article in question. "If you glance at it you will see how exquisitely it is carved."

Concealing his eagerness with an effort, Simon Carne drew his chair up to the table, and examined the box.

It was with justice she had described it as a work of art. What the wood was of which it was constructed Carne was unable to tell. It was dark and heavy, and, though it was not teak, closely resembled it. It was literally covered with quaint carving, and of its kind was an unique work of art.

"It is most curious and beautiful," said Carne when he had finished his examination. "In all my experience I can safely say I have never seen its equal. If you will permit me I should very much like to include a description and an illustration of it in my book."

"Of course you may do so; I shall be only too delighted," answered Her Grace. "If it will help you in your work I shall be glad to lend it to you for a few hours, in order that you may have the illustration made."

This was exactly what Carne had been waiting for, and he accepted the offer with alacrity.

"Very well, then," she said. "On the day of my ball, when it will be brought from the bank again, I will take the necklace out and send the case to you. I must make one proviso, however, and that is that you let me have it back the same day."

"I will certainly promise to do that," replied Carne.

"And now let us look inside," said his hostess.

Choosing a key from a bunch she carried in her pocket, she unlocked the casket, and lifted the lid. Accustomed as Carne had all his life been to the sight of gems, what he then saw before him almost took his breath away. The inside of the box, both sides and bottom, was quilted with the softest Russia leather, and on this luxurious couch reposed the famous necklace. The fire of the stones when the light caught them was sufficient to dazzle the eyes, so fierce was it.

As Carne could see, every gem was perfect of its kind, and there were no fewer than three hundred of them. The setting was a fine example of the jeweller's art, and last, but not least, the value of the whole affair was fifty thousand pounds, a mere fleabite to the man who had given it to his wife, but a fortune to any humbler person.

"And now that you have seen my property, what do you think of it?" asked the Duchess as she watched her visitor's face.

"It is very beautiful," he answered, "and I do not wonder that you are proud of it. Yes, the diamonds are very fine, but I think it is their abiding place that fascinates me more. Have you any objection to my measuring it?"

"Pray do so, if it is likely to be of any assistance to you," replied Her Grace.

Carne thereupon produced a small ivory rule, ran it over the box, and the figures he thus obtained he jotted down in his pocket-book.

Ten minutes later, when the case had been returned to the safe, he thanked the Duchess for her kindness and took his departure, promising to call in person for the empty case on the morning of the ball.

Reaching home he passed into his study, and, seating himself at his writing table, pulled a sheet of note paper towards him and began to sketch, as well as he could remember it, the box he had seen. Then he leant back in his chair and closed his eyes.

"I have cracked a good many hard nuts in my time," he said reflectively, "but never one that seemed so difficult at first sight as this. As far as I see at present, the case stands as follows: the box will be brought from the bank where it usually reposes to Wiltshire House on the morning of the dance. I shall be allowed to have possession of it, without the stones of course, for a period possibly extending from eleven o'clock in the morning to four or five, at any rate not later than seven, in the evening. After the ball the necklace will be returned to it, when it will be locked up in the safe, over which the butler and a footman will mount guard.

"To get into the room during the night is not only too risky, but physically out of the question; while to rob Her Grace of her treasure during the progress of the dance would be equally impossible. The Duke fetches the casket and takes it back to the bank himself, so that to all intents and purposes I am almost as far off the solution as ever."

Half an hour went by and found him still seated at his desk, staring at the drawing on the paper, then an hour. The traffic of the streets rolled past the house unheeded. Finally Jowur Singh announced his carriage, and, feeling that an idea might come to him with a change of scene, he set off for a drive in the park.

By this time his elegant mail phaeton, with its magnificent horses and Indian servant on the seat behind, was as well-known as Her Majesty's state equipage, and attracted almost as much attention. To-day, however, the fashionable world noticed that Simon Carne looked preoccupied. He was still working out his problem, but so far without much success. Suddenly something, no one will ever be able to say what, put an idea into his head. The notion was no sooner born in his brain than he left the park and drove quickly home. Ten minutes had scarcely elapsed before he was back in his study again, and had ordered that Wajib Baksh should be sent to him.

When the man he wanted put in an appearance, Carne handed him the paper upon which he had made the drawing of the jewel case.

"Look at that," he said, "and tell me what thou seest there."

"I see a box," answered the man, who by this time was well accustomed to his master's ways.

"As thou say'st, it is a box," said Carne. "The wood is heavy and thick, though what wood it is I do not know. The measurements are upon the paper below. Within, both the sides and bottom are quilted with soft leather, as I have also shown. Think now, Wajib Baksh, for in this case thou wilt need to have all thy wits about thee. Tell me is it in thy power, oh most cunning of all craftsmen, to insert such extra sides within this box that they, being held by a spring, shall lie so snug as not to be noticeable to the ordinary eye? Can it be so arranged that, when the box is locked, they shall fall flat upon the bottom, thus covering and holding fast what lies beneath them, and yet making the box appear to the eye as if it were empty. Is it possible for thee to do such a thing?"

Wajib Baksh did not reply for a few moments. His instinct told him what his master wanted, and he was not disposed to answer hastily, for he also saw that his reputation as the most cunning craftsman in India was at stake.

"If the Heaven-born will permit me the night for thought," he said at last, "I will come to him when he rises from his bed and tell him what I can do, and he can then give his orders as it pleases him."

"Very good," said Carne. "Then to-morrow morning I shall expect thy report. Let the work be good, and there will be many rupees for thee to touch in return. As to the lock and the way it shall act, let that be the concern of Hiram Singh."

Wajib Baksh salaamed and withdrew, and Simon Carne for the time being dismissed the matter from his mind.

Next morning, while he was dressing, Belton reported that the two artificers desired an interview with him. He ordered them to be admitted, and forthwith they entered the room. It was noticeable that Wajib Baksh carried in his hand a heavy box, which, upon Carne's motioning him to do so, he placed upon the table.

"Have ye thought over the matter?" he asked, seeing that the men waited for him to speak.

"We have thought of it," replied Hiram Singh, who always acted as spokesman for the pair. "If the Presence will deign to look, he will see that we have made a box of the size and shape such as he drew upon the paper."

"Yes, it is certainly a good copy," said Carne condescendingly, after he had examined it.

Wajib Baksh showed his white teeth in appreciation of the compliment, and Hiram Singh drew closer to the table.

"And now, if the Sahib will open it, he will in his wisdom be able to tell if it resembles the other that he has in his mind."

Carne opened the box as requested, and discovered that the interior was an exact counterfeit of the Duchess of Wiltshire's jewel case, even to the extent of the quilted leather lining which had been the other's principal feature. He admitted that the likeness was all that could be desired.

"As he is satisfied," said Hiram Singh, "it may be that the Protector of the Poor will deign to try an experiment with it. See, here is a comb. Let it be placed in the box, so— now he will see what he will see."

The broad, silver-backed comb, lying upon his dressing-table, was placed on the bottom of the box, the lid was closed, and the key turned in the lock. The case being securely fastened, Hiram Singh laid it before his master.

"I am to open it, I suppose?" said Carne, taking the key and replacing it in the lock.

"If my master pleases," replied the other.

Carne accordingly turned it in the lock, and, having done so, raised the lid and looked inside. His astonishment was complete. To all intents and purposes the box was empty. The comb was not to be seen, and yet the quilted sides and bottom were, to all appearances, just the same as when he had first looked inside.

"This is most wonderful," he said. And indeed it was as clever a conjuring trick as any he had ever seen.

"Nay, it is very simple," Wajib Baksh replied. "The Heaven-born told me that there must be no risk of detection."

He took the box in his own hands and, running his nails down the centre of the quilting, dividing the false bottom into two pieces; these he lifted out, revealing the comb lying upon the real bottom beneath.

"The sides, as my lord will see," said Hiram Singh, taking a step forward, "are held in their appointed places by these two springs. Thus, when the key is turned the springs relax, and the sides are driven by others into their places on the bottom, where the seams in the quilting mask the join. There is but one disadvantage. It is as follows: When the pieces which form the bottom are lifted out in order that my lord may get at whatever lies concealed beneath, the springs must of necessity stand revealed. However, to any one who knows sufficient of the working of the box to lift out the false bottom, it will be an easy matter to withdraw the springs and conceal them about his person."

"As you say that is an easy matter," said Carne, "and I shall not be likely to forget. Now one other question. Presuming I am in a position to put the real box into your hands for say eight hours, do you think that in that time you can fit it up so that detection will be impossible?"

"Assuredly, my lord," replied Hiram Singh with conviction. "There is but the lock and the fitting of the springs to be done. Three hours at most would suffice for that."

"I am pleased with you," said Carne. "As a proof of my satisfaction, when the work is finished you will each receive five hundred rupees. Now you can go."

According to his promise, ten o'clock on the Friday following found him in his hansom driving towards Belgrave Square. He was a little anxious, though the casual observer would scarcely have been able to tell it. The magnitude of the stake for which he was playing was enough to try the nerve of even such a past master in his profession as Simon Carne.

Arriving at the house he discovered some workmen erecting

an awning across the footway in preparation for the ball that was to take place at night. It was not long, however, before he found himself in the boudoir, reminding Her Grace of her promise to permit him an opportunity of making a drawing of the famous jewel case. The Duchess was naturally busy, and within a quarter of an hour he was on his way home with the box placed on the seat of the carriage beside him.

"Now," he said, as he patted it good-humouredly, "if only the notion worked out by Hiram Singh and Wajib Baksh holds good, the famous Wiltshire diamonds will become my property before very many hours are passed. By this time tomorrow, I suppose, London will be all agog concerning the burglary."

On reaching his house he left his carriage, and himself carried the box into his study. Once there he rang his bell and ordered Hiram Singh and Wajib Baksh to be sent to him. When they arrived he showed them the box upon which they were to exercise their ingenuity.

"Bring your tools in here," he said, "and do the work under my own eyes. You have but nine hours before you, so you must make the most of them."

The men went for their implements, and as soon as they were ready set to work. All through the day they were kept hard at it, with the result that by five o'clock the alterations had been effected and the case stood ready. By the time Carne returned from his afternoon drive in the Park it was quite prepared for the part it was to play in his scheme. Having praised the men, he turned them out and locked the door, then went across the room and unlocked a drawer in his writing table. From it he took a flat leather jewel case, which he opened. It contained a necklace of counterfeit diamonds, if anything a little larger than the one he intended to try to obtain. He had purchased it that morning in the Burlington Arcade for the purpose of testing the apparatus his servants had made, and this he now proceeded to do.

Laying it carefully upon the bottom he closed the lid and turned the key. When he opened it again the necklace was gone, and even though he knew the secret he could not for the life of him see where the false bottom began and ended. After that he reset the trap and tossed the necklace carelessly in. To his delight it acted as well as on the previous occasion. He could scarcely contain his satisfaction. His conscience was sufficiently elastic to give him no trouble. To him it was scarcely a robbery he was planning, but an artistic trial of skill, in which he pitted his wits and cunning against the forces of society in general.

At half-past seven he dined, and afterwards smoked a meditative cigar over the evening paper in the billiard room. The invitations to the ball were for ten o'clock, and at nine-thirty he went to his dressing-room.

"Make me tidy as quickly as you can," he said to Belton when the latter appeared, "and while you are doing so listen to my final instructions."

"To-night, as you know, I am endeavouring to secure the Duchess of Wiltshire's necklace. To-morrow morning all London will resound with the hubbub, and I have been making my plans in such a way as to arrange that Klimo shall be the first person consulted. When the messenger calls, if call he does, see that the old woman next door bids him tell the Duke to come personally at twelve o'clock. Do you understand?"

"Perfectly, sir?"

"Very good. Now give me the jewel case, and let me be off. You need not sit up for me."

Precisely as the clocks in the neighbourhood were striking ten Simon Carne reached Belgrave Square, and, as he hoped, found himself the first guest.

His hostess and her husband received him in the ante-room of the drawing-room.

"I come laden with a thousand apologies," he said as he took Her Grace's hand, and bent over it with that ceremonious politeness which was one of the man's chief characteristics. "I am most unconscionably early, I know, but I hastened here in order that I might personally return the jewel case you so kindly lent me. I must trust to your generosity to forgive me. The drawings took longer than I expected."

"Please do not apologise," answered Her Grace. "It is very

kind of you to have brought the case yourself. I hope the illustrations have proved successful. I shall look forward to seeing
them as soon as they are ready. But I am keeping you holding
the box. One of my servants will take it to my room."

She called a footman to her, and bade him take the box and
place it upon her dressing-table.

"Before it goes I must let you see that I have not damaged it
either externally or internally," said Carne with a laugh. "It is
such a valuable case that I should never forgive myself if it had
even received a scratch during the time it has been in my possession."

So saying he lifted the lid and allowed her to look inside. To
all appearance it was exactly the same as when she had lent it
to him earlier in the day.

"You have been most careful," she said. And then, with an
air of banter, she continued: "If you desire it, I shall be pleased
to give you a certificate to that effect."

They jested in this fashion for a few moments after the servant's departure, during which time Carne promised to call
upon her the following morning at 11 o'clock, and to bring
with him the illustrations he had made and a queer little piece
of china he had had the good fortune to pick up in a dealer's
shop the previous afternoon. By this time fashionable London
was making its way up the grand staircase, and with its
appearance further conversation became impossible.

Shortly after midnight Carne bade his hostess good-night
and slipped away. He was perfectly satisfied with his evening's
entertainment, and if the key of the jewel case were not turned
before the jewels were placed in it, he was convinced they
would become his property. It speaks well for his strength of
nerve when I record the fact that on going to bed his slumbers
were as peaceful and untroubled as those of a little child.

Breakfast was scarcely over next morning before a hansom
drew up at his front door and Lord Amberley alighted. He was
ushered into Carne's presence forthwith, and on seeing that
the latter was surprised at his early visit, hastened to explain.

"My dear fellow," he said, as he took possession of the chair
the other offered him, "I have come round to see you on most

important business. As I told you last night at the dance, when you so kindly asked me to come and see the steam yacht you have purchased, I had an appointment with Wiltshire at half-past nine this morning. On reaching Belgrave Square, I found the whole house in confusion. Servants were running hither and thither with scared faces, the butler was on the borders of lunacy, the Duchess was well-nigh hysterical in her boudoir, while her husband was in his study vowing vengeance against all the world."

"You alarm me," said Carne, lighting a cigarette with a hand that was as steady as a rock. "What on earth has happened?"

"I think I might safely allow you fifty guesses and then wager a hundred pounds you'd not hit the mark; and yet in a certain measure it concerns you."

"Concerns me? Good gracious! What have I done to bring all this about?"

"Pray do not look so alarmed," said Amberley. Personally you have done nothing. Indeed, on second thoughts, I don't know that I am right in saying that it concerns you at all. The fact of the matter is, Carne, a burglary took place last night at Wiltshire House, *and the famous necklace has disappeared.*"

"Good heavens! You don't say so?"

"But I *do.* The circumstances of the case are as follows: When my cousin retired to her room last night after the ball, she unclasped the necklace, and, in her husband's presence, placed it carefully in her jewel case, which she locked. That having been done, Wiltshire took the box to the room which contained the safe, and himself placed it there, locking the iron door with his own key. The room was occupied that night, according to custom, by the butler and one of the footmen, both of whom have been in the family since they were boys.

"Next morning, after breakfast, the Duke unlocked the safe and took out the box, intending to convey it to the Bank as usual. Before leaving, however, he placed it on his study-table and went upstairs to speak to his wife. He cannot remember exactly how long he was absent, but he feels convinced that he was not gone more than a quarter of an hour at the very utmost.

"Their conversation finished, she accompanied him downstairs, where she saw him take up the case to carry it to his carriage. Before he left the house, however, she said: 'I suppose you have looked to see that the necklace is all right?' 'How could I do so?' was his reply. 'You know you possess the only key that will fit it?'

"She felt in her pockets, but to her surprise the key was not there."

"If I were a detective I should say that that is a point to be remembered," said Carne with a smile. "Pray, where did she find her keys?"

"Upon her dressing-table," said Amberley. "Though she has not the slightest recollection of leaving them there."

"Well, when she had procured the keys, what happened?"

"Why, they opened the box, and, to their astonishment and dismay, *found it empty. The jewels were gone!*"

"Good gracious! What a terrible loss! It seems almost impossible that it can be true. And pray, what did they do?"

"At first they stood staring into the empty box, hardly believing the evidence of their own eyes. Stare how they would, however, they could not bring them back. The jewels had, without doubt, disappeared, but when and where the robbery had taken place it was impossible to say. After that they had up all the servants and questioned them, but the result was what they might have foreseen, no one from the butler to the kitchenmaid could throw any light upon the subject. To this minute it remains as great a mystery as when they first discovered it."

"I am more concerned than I can tell you," said Carne. "How thankful I ought to be that I returned the case to Her Grace last night. But in thinking of myself I am forgetting to ask what has brought you to me. If I can be of any assistance I hope you will command me."

"Well, I'll tell you why I have come," replied Lord Amberley. "Naturally, they are most anxious to have the mystery solved and the jewels recovered as soon as possible. Wiltshire wanted to send to Scotland Yard there and then, but his wife and I eventually persuaded him to consult Klimo. As you know, if the police authorities are called in first, he refuses the business altogether. Now, we thought, as you are his next door neighbour, you might possibly be able to assist us."

"You may be very sure, my lord, I will do everything that lies in my power. Let us go in and see him at once."

As he spoke he rose and threw what remained of his cigarette into the fireplace. His visitor having imitated his example, they procured their hats and walked round from Park Lane into Belverton Street to bring up at No. 1. After they had rung the bell the door was opened to them by the old woman who invariably received the detective's clients.

"Is Mr. Klimo at home?" asked Carne. "And if so, can we see him?"

The old lady was a little deaf, and the question had to be repeated before she could be made to understand what was wanted. As soon, however, as she realized their desire, she informed them that her master was absent from town, but would be back as usual at twelve o'clock to meet his clients.

"What on earth's to be done?" said the Earl, looking at his companion in dismay. "I am afraid I can't come back again, as I have a most important appointment at that hour."

"Do you think you could entrust the business to me?" asked Carne. "If so, I will make a point of seeing him at twelve o'clock, and could call at Wiltshire House afterwards and tell the Duke what I have done."

"That's very good of you," replied Amberley. "If you are sure it would not put you to too much trouble, that would be quite the best thing to be done."

"I will do it with pleasure," Carne replied. "I feel it my duty to help in whatever way I can."

"You are very kind," said the other. "Then, as I understand it, you are to call upon Klimo at twelve o'clock, and afterwards to let my cousins know what you have succeeded in doing. I only hope he will help us to secure the thief. We are having too many of these burglaries just now. I must catch this hansom and be off. Good-bye, and many thanks."

"Good-bye," said Carne, and shook him by the hand.

The hansom having rolled away, Carne retraced his steps to his own abode.

"It is really very strange," he muttered as he walked along, "how often chance condescends to lend her assistance to my little schemes. The mere fact that His Grace left the box unwatched in his study for a quarter of an hour may serve to throw the police off on quite another scent. I am also glad that they decided to open the case in the house, for if it had gone to the bankers' and had been placed in the strong room unexamined, I should never have been able to get possession of the jewels at all."

Three hours later he drove to Wiltshire House and saw the Duke. The Duchess was far too much upset by the catastrophe to see any one.

"This is really most kind of you, Mr. Carne," said His Grace when the other had supplied an elaborate account of his interview with Klimo. "We are extremely indebted to you. I am sorry he cannot come before ten o'clock to-night, and that he makes this stipulation of my seeing him alone, for I must confess I should like to have had some one else present to ask any questions that might escape me. But if that's his usual hour and custom, well, we must abide by it, that's all. I hope he will do some good, for this is the greatest calamity that has ever befallen me. As I told you just now, it has made my wife quite ill. She is confined to her bedroom and quite hysterical."

"You do not suspect any one, I suppose?" inquired Carne.

"Not a soul," the other answered. "The thing is such a mystery that we do not know what to think. I feel convinced, however, that my servants are as innocent as I am. Nothing will ever make me think them otherwise. I wish I could catch the fellow, that's all. I'd make him suffer for the trick he's played me."

Carne offered an appropriate reply, and after a little further conversation upon the subject, bade the irate nobleman goodbye and left the house. From Belgrave Square he drove to one of the clubs of which he had been elected a member, in search of Lord Orpington, with whom he had promised to lunch, and afterwards took him to a ship-builder's yard near Greenwich, in order to show him the steam yacht he had lately purchased.

It was close upon dinner time before he returned to his own residence. He brought Lord Orpington with him, and they dined in state together. At nine the latter bade him good-bye, and at ten Carne retired to his dressing-room and rang for Belton.

"What have you to report," he asked, "with regard to what I bade you do in Belgrave Square?"

"I followed your instructions to the letter," Belton replied. "Yesterday morning I wrote to Messrs. Horniblow and Jimson, the house agents in Piccadilly, in the name of Colonel Braithwaite, and asked for an order to view the residence to the right of Wiltshire House. I asked that the order might be sent direct to the house, where the Colonel would get it upon his arrival. This letter I posted myself in Basingstoke, as you desired me to do.

"At nine o'clock yesterday morning I dressed myself as much like an elderly army officer as possible, and took a cab to Belgrave Square. The caretaker, an old fellow of close upon seventy years of age, admitted me immediately upon hearing my name, and proposed that he should show me over the house. This, however, I told him was quite unnecessary, backing my speech with a present of half a crown, whereupon he returned to his breakfast perfectly satisfied, while I wandered about the house at my own leisure.

"Reaching the same floor as that upon which is situated the room in which the Duke's safe is kept, I discovered that your supposition was quite correct, and that it would be possible for a man, by opening the window, to make his way along the coping from one house to the other, without being seen. I made certain that there was no one in the bedroom in which the butler slept, and then arranged the long telescope walking-stick you gave me, and fixed one of my boots to it by means of the screw in the end. With this I was able to make a regular succession of footsteps in the dust along the ledge, between one window and the other.

"That done, I went downstairs again, bade the caretaker good-morning, and got into my cab. From Belgrave Square I drove to the shop of the pawnbroker whom you told me you had discovered was out of town. His assistant inquired my business, and was anxious to do what he could for me. I told him, however, that I must see his master personally, as it was about the sale of some diamonds I had had left me. I pretended to be annoyed that he was not at home, and muttered to myself, so that the man could hear, something about its meaning a journey to Amsterdam.

"Then I limped out of the shop, paid off my cab, and, walking down a by-street, removed my moustache, and altered my appearance by taking off my great coat and muffler. A few streets further on I purchased a bowler hat in place of the old-fashioned topper I had hitherto been wearing, and then took a cab from Piccadilly and came home."

"You have fulfilled my instructions admirably," said Carne. "And if the business comes off, as I expect it will, you shall receive your usual percentage. Now I must be turned into Klimo and be off to Belgrave Square to put His Grace of Wiltshire upon the track of this burglar."

Before he retired to rest that night Simon Carne took something, wrapped in a red silk handkerchief, from the capacious pocket of the coat Klimo had been wearing a few moments before. Having unrolled the covering, he held up to the light the magnificent necklace which for so many years had been the joy and pride of the ducal house of Wiltshire. The electric light played upon it, and touched it with a thousand different hues."

"Where so many have failed," he said to himself, as he wrapped it in the handkerchief again and locked it in his safe, "it is pleasant to be able to congratulate oneself on having succeeded. It is without its equal, and I don't think I shall be over-stepping the mark if I say that I think when she receives it Liz will be glad she lent me the money."

Next morning all London was astonished by the news that the famous Wiltshire diamonds had been stolen, and a few hours later Carne learnt from an evening paper that the detectives who had taken up the case, upon the supposed retirement from it of Klimo, were still completely at fault.

That evening he was to entertain several friends to dinner. They included Lord Amberley, Lord Orpington, and a prominent member of the Privy Council. Lord Amberley arrived late, but filled to overflowing with importance. His friends noticed his state, and questioned him.

"Well, gentlemen," he answered, as he took up a commanding position upon the drawing-room hearthrug, "I am in a position to inform you that Klimo has reported upon the case, and the upshot of it is that the Wiltshire Diamond Mystery is a mystery no longer."

"What do you mean?" asked the others in a chorus.

"I mean that he sent in his report to Wiltshire this afternoon, as arranged. From what he said the other night, after being alone in the room with the empty jewel case and a magnifying glass for two minutes or so, he was in a position to describe the *modus operandi*, and, what is more, to put the police on the scent of the burglar."

"And how *was* it worked?" asked Carne.

"From the empty house next door," replied the other. "On the morning of the burglary a man, purporting to be a retired army officer, called with an order to view, got the caretaker out of the way, clambered along to Wiltshire House by means of the parapet outside, reached the room during the time the servants were at breakfast, opened the safe, and abstracted the jewels."

"But how did Klimo find all this out?" asked Lord Orpington.

"By his own inimitable cleverness," replied Lord Amberley. "At any rate it has been proved that he was correct. The man *did* make his way from next door, and the police have since discovered that an individual, answering to the description given, visited a pawnbroker's shop in the city about an hour later, and stated that he had diamonds to sell."

"If that is so it turns out to be a very simple mystery after all," said Lord Orpington as they began their meal.

"Thanks to the ingenuity of the cleverest detective in the world," remarked Amberley.

"In that case here's a good health to Klimo," said the Privy Councillor, raising his glass.

"I will join you in that," said Simon Carne. "Here's a very good health to Klimo and his connection with the Duchess of Wiltshire's diamonds. May he always be equally successful!"

"Hear, hear to that," replied his guests.

CHAPTER 2

HOW SIMON CARNE WON THE DERBY

It was seven o'clock on one of the brightest mornings of all that year. The scene was Waterloo Station, where the Earl of Amberley, Lord Orpington, and the Marquis of Laverstock were pacing up and down the main line departure platform, gazing anxiously about them. It was evident, from the way they scrutinised every person who approached them, that they were on the look-out for some one. This some one ultimately proved to be Simon Carne, who, when he appeared, greeted them with considerable cordiality, at the same time apologising for his lateness in joining them.

"I think this must be our train," he said, pointing to the carriages drawn up beside the platform on which they stood. "At any rate, here is my man. By dint of study he has turned himself into a sort of walking Bradshaw, and he will certainly be able to inform us."

The inimitable Belton deferentially insinuated that his master was right in his conjecture, and then led the way towards a Pullman car, which had been attached to the train for the convenience of Carne and his guests. They took their seats, and a few moments later the train moved slowly out of the station. Carne was in the best of spirits, and the fact that he was taking his friends down to the stables of his trainer, William Bent, in order that they might witness a trial of his candidate for the Derby, seemed to give him the greatest possible pleasure.

On reaching Merford, the little wayside station nearest the village in which the training stables were situated, they discovered a comfortable four-wheeled conveyance drawn up to receive them. The driver touched his hat, and stated that his master was awaiting them on the Downs; this proved to be the case, for when they left the high road and turned on to the soft turf they saw before them a string of thoroughbreds, and the trainer himself mounted upon his well-known white pony, Columbine.

"Good-morning, Bent," said Carne, as the latter rode up and lifted his hat to himself and friends. "You see we have kept our promise, and are here to witness the trial you said you had arranged for us."

"I am glad to see you, sir," Bent replied. "And I only hope that what I am about to show you will prove of service to you. The horse is as fit as mortal hands can make him, and if he don't do his best for you next week there will be one person surprised in England, and that one will be myself. As you know, sir, the only horse I dread is Vulcanite, and the fact cannot be denied that he's a real clinker."

"Well," said Carne, "when we have seen our animal gallop we shall know better how much trust we are to place in him. For my own part I'm not afraid. Vulcanite, as you say, is a good horse, but, if I'm not mistaken, Knight of Malta is a better. Surely this is he coming towards us."

"That's him," said the trainer, with a fine disregard for grammar. "There's no mistaking him, is there? And now, if you'd care to stroll across we'll see them saddle."

The party accordingly descended from the carriage, and walked across the turf to the spot where the four thoroughbreds were being divested of their sheets. They made a pretty group; but even the most inexperienced critic could scarcely have failed to pick out Knight of Malta as the best among them. He was a tall, shapely bay, with black points, a trifle light of flesh perhaps, but with clean, flat legs, and low, greyhound-like thighs, sure evidence of the enormous propelling power he was known to possess. His head was perfection itself, though a wee bit too lop-eared if anything. Taken altogether, he looked, what he was, thoroughbred every inch of him. The others of the party were Gasometer, Hydrogen, and Young Romeo, the

last named being the particular trial horse of the party. It was a
favourite boast of the trainer that the last named was so reli-
able in his habits, his condition, and his pace, that you would
not be far wrong if you were to set your watch by him.

"By the way, Bent," said Carne, as the boys were lifted into
their saddles, "what weights are the horses carrying?"

"Well, sir, Young Romeo carries 8st. 9lb.; Gasometer, 7st.
8lb.; Hydrogen, 7st. 1lb.; and the Knight, 9st. 11lb. The distance will be the Epsom course, one mile and a half, and the
best horse to win. Now, sir, if you're ready we'll get to work."

He turned to the lad who was to ride Hydrogen.

"Once you are off you will make the running, and bring
them along at your best pace to the dip, where Gasometer will,
if possible, take it up. After that I leave it to you other boys to
make the best race of it you can. You, Blunt," calling up his
head lad, "go down with them to the post, and get them off to
as good a start as possible."

The horses departed, and Simon Carne and his friends
accompanied the trainer to a spot where they would see the
finish to the best advantage. Five minutes later an ejaculation
from Lord Orpington told them that the horses had started.
Each man accordingly clapped his glasses to his eyes, and
watched the race before them. Faithful to his instructions, the
lad on Hydrogen came straight to the front, and led them a
cracker until they descended into the slight dip which marked
the end of the first half-mile.

Then he retired to the rear, hopelessly done for, and Gasometer took up the running, with Knight of Malta close alongside him, and Young Romeo only half a length away. As they
passed the mile post Young Romeo shot to the front, but it
soon became evident he had not come to stay. Good horse as
he was, there was a better catching him hand over fist. The
pace was all that could be desired, and when Knight of Malta
swept past the group, winner of the trial by more than his own
length, the congratulations Simon Carne received were as cor-
dial as he could possibly desire.

"What did I tell you, sir?" said Bent, with a smile of satisfaction upon his face. "You see what a good horse he is. There's no mistake about that."

"Well, let us hope he will do as well a week hence," Carne replied simply, as he replaced his glasses in their case.

"Amen to that," remarked Lord Orpington.

"And now, gentlemen," said the trainer, "if you will allow me, I will drive you over to my place to breakfast."

They took their places in the carriage once more, and, Bent having taken the reins, in a few moments they were bowling along the high road towards a neat modern residence standing on a slight eminence on the edge of the Downs. This was the trainer's own place of abode, the stables containing his many precious charges lying a hundred yards or so to the rear.

They were received on the threshold by the trainer's wife, who welcomed them most heartily to Merford. The keen air of the Downs had sharpened their appetites, and when they sat down to table they found they were able to do full justice to the excellent fare provided for them. The meal at an end, they inspected the stables, once more carefully examining the Derby candidate, who seemed none the worse for his morning's exertion, and then Carne left his guests in the big yard to the enjoyment of their cigars, while he accompanied his trainer into the house for a few moments' chat.

"And now sit down, sir," said Bent, when they reached his own sanctum, a cosy apartment, half sitting-room and half office, bearing upon its walls innumerable mementoes of circumstances connected with the owner's lengthy turf experiences. "I hope you are satisfied with what you saw this morning?"

"Perfectly satisfied," said Carne, "but I should like to hear exactly what you think about the race itself."

"Well, sir, as you may imagine, I have been thinking a good deal about it lately, and this is the conclusion I have come to. If this were an ordinary year, I should say that we possess out and away the best horse in the race; but we must remember that this is not by any means an ordinary year—there's Vulcanite, who they tell me is in the very pink of condition, and who has beaten our horse each time they have met; there's the

Mandarin, who won the Two Thousand this week, and who will be certain to come into greater favour as the time shortens, and The Filibuster, who won the Biennial Stakes at the Craven Meeting, a nice enough horse, though I must say I don't fancy him over much myself."

"I take it, then, that the only horse you really fear is Vulcanite?"

"That's so, sir. If he were not in the list, I should feel as certain of seeing you leading your horse back a winner as any man could well be."

On looking at his watch Carne discovered that it was time for him to rejoin his friends and be off to the railway station if they desired to catch the train which they had arranged should convey them back to town. So bidding the trainer and his wife good-bye, they took their places in the carriage once more, and were driven away.

Arriving at Waterloo, they drove to Lord Orpington's club to lunch.

"Do you know you're a very lucky fellow, Carne?" said the Earl of Amberley as they stood on the steps of that institution afterwards, before separating in pursuit of the pleasures of the afternoon. "You have health, wealth, fame, good looks, one of the finest houses in London, and now one of the prospective winners of the Derby. In fact, you only want one thing to make your existence perfect."

"And what is that?" asked Carne.

"A wife," replied Lord Amberley. "I wonder the girls have let you escape so long."

"I am not a marrying man," said Carne; "how could a fellow like myself, who is here to-day and gone to-morrow, expect any woman to link her lot with his? Do you remember our first meeting?"

"Perfectly," replied Lord Amberley. "When I close my eyes I can see that beautiful marble palace, set in its frame of blue water, as plainly as if it were but yesterday I breakfasted with you there."

"That was a very fortunate morning for me," said the other. "And now here is my cab. I must be off. Good-bye."

"Good-bye," cried his friends, as he went down the steps and entered the vehicle. "Don't forget to let us know if anything further turns up."

"I will be sure to do so," said Simon Carne, and then, as he laid himself back on the soft cushions and was driven by way of Waterloo Place to Piccadilly, he added to himself, "Yes, if I can bring off the little scheme I have in my mind, and one or two others which I am preparing, and can manage to get out of England without any one suspecting that I am the burglar who has outwitted all London, I shall have good cause to say that was a *very* fortunate day for me when I first met his lordship."

That evening he dined alone. He seemed pre-occupied, and it was evident that he was disappointed about something. Several times on hearing noises in the street outside he questioned his servants as to the cause. At last, however, when Ram Gafur entered the room carrying a telegram upon a salver, his feelings found vent in a sigh of satisfaction. With eager fingers he broke open the envelope, withdrew the contents, and read the message it contained:

"Seven Stars Music Hall—Whitechapel Road. Ten o'clock."

There was no signature, but that fact did not seem to trouble him very much. He placed it in his pocket-book, and afterwards continued his meal in better spirits. When the servants had left the room he poured himself out a glass of port, and taking a pencil proceeded to make certain calculations upon the back of an envelope. For nearly ten minutes he occupied himself in this way, then he tore the paper into tiny pieces, replaced his pencil in his pocket, and sipped his wine with a satisfaction that was the outcome of perfected arrangements.

"The public excitement," he said to himself, not without a small touch of pride, "has as yet scarcely cooled down from the robbery of the famous Wiltshire jewels. Lord Orpington has not as yet discovered the whereabouts of the gold and silver plate which disappeared from his house so mysteriously a week or two ago, while several other people have done their best to catch a gang of burglars who would seem to have set all London at defiance. But if I bring off this new *coup*, they'll forget all their grievances in consideration of the latest and greatest scandal. There'll be scarcely a man in England who won't have something to say upon the subject. By the way, let me see how he stands in the betting to-night."

He took a paper from the table in the window, and glanced down the sporting column. Vulcanite was evidently the public's choice, Knight of Malta being only second favourite, with the Mandarin a strong third.

"What a hubbub there will be when it becomes known," said Carne, as he placed the paper on the table again. "I shall have to take especial care, or some of the storm may blow back on me. I fancy I can hear the newsboys shouting: 'Latest news of the turf scandal. The Derby favourite stolen. Vulcanite missing. An attempt made to get at Knight of Malta.' Why! It will be twenty years before old England will forget the sensation I am about to give her."

With a grim chuckle at the idea, he went upstairs to his dressing-room and locked the door. It must have been well after nine o'clock when he emerged again, and, clad in a long ulster, left the house in his private hansom. Passing down Park Lane he drove along Piccadilly, then by way of the Haymarket, Strand, Ludgate Hill, and Fenchurch Street to the Whitechapel Road. Reaching the corner of Leman Street, he signalled to his man to stop, and jumped out.

His appearance was now entirely changed. Instead of the deformed, scholar-like figure he usually presented, he now resembled a common-place, farmerish individual, with iron grey hair, a somewhat crafty face, ornamented with bushy eyebrows and a quantity of fluffy whiskers. How he had managed it as he drove along goodness only knows, but that he had effected the change was certain.

Having watched his cab drive away, he strolled along the street until he arrived at a building, the flaring lights of which proclaimed it the Seven Stars Music Hall. He paid his money at the box office, and then walked inside to find a fair-sized building, upon the floor of which were placed possibly a hundred small tables. On the stage at the further end a young lady, boasting a minimum of clothing and a maximum of self-assurance, was explaining, to the dashing accompaniment of the orchestra, the adventures she had experienced "When Billy and me was courting."

Acting up to his appearance, Carne called for a "two of Scotch cold," and, having lit a meerschaum pipe which he took from his waistcoat pocket, prepared to make himself at home. As ten o'clock struck he turned his chair a little, in order that he might have a better view of the door, and waited.

Five minutes must have elapsed before his patience was rewarded. Then two men came in together, and immediately he saw them he turned his face in an opposite direction, and seemed to be taking an absorbing interest in what was happening upon the stage.

One of the men who had entered, and whom he had seemed to recognise—a cadaverous-looking individual in a suit of clothes a size too small for him, a velvet waistcoat at least three sizes too large, a check tie, in which was stuck an enormous horseshoe pin composed of palpably imitation diamonds, boasting no shirt as far as could be seen, and wearing upon his head a top hat of a shape that had been fashionable in the early sixties—stopped, and placed his hand upon his shoulder.

"Mr. Blenkins, or I'm a d'isy," he said. "Well, who'd ha' thought of seeing you here of all places? Why, it was only this afternoon as me and my friend, Mr. Brown here, was a-speaking of you. To think as how you should ha' come up to London just this very time, and be at the Seven Stars Music Hall, of all other places! It's like what the noospapers call a go-insidence, drat me if it ain't. 'Ow are yer, old pal?"

He extended his hand, which Mr. Blenkins took, and shook with considerable cordiality. After that, Mr. Brown, who from outward appearances was by far the most respectable of the trio, was introduced in the capacity of a gentleman from America, a citizenship that became more apparent when he opened his mouth to speak.

"And what was 'ee speaking of I about?" asked Mr. Blenkins, when the trio were comfortably seated at table.

This the diffident Mr. Jones, for by that commonplace appellative the seedy gentleman with the magnificent diamonds chose to be called, declined to state. It would appear that he was willing to discuss the news of the day, the price of forage, the prospects of war, the programme proceeding upon the stage, in fact, anything rather than declare the subject of his conversation with Mr. Brown that afternoon.

It was not until Mr. Brown happened to ask Mr. Blenkins what horse he fancied for the Derby that Mr. Jones in any degree recovered his self-possession. Then an animated discussion on the forthcoming race was entered upon. How long it would have lasted had not Mr. Jones presently declared that the music of the orchestra was too much for him, I cannot say.

Thereupon Mr. Brown suggested that they should leave the Hall and proceed to a place of which he knew in a neighbouring street. This they accordingly did, and when they were safely installed in a small room off the bar, Mr. Jones, having made certain that there was no one near enough to overhear, unlocked his powers of conversation with whisky and water, and proceeded to speak his mind.

For upwards of an hour they remained closeted in the room together, conversing in an undertone. Then the meeting broke up, Mr. Blenkins bidding his friends "good-night" before they left the house.

From the outward appearances of the party, if in these days of seedy millionaires and overdressed bankrupts one may venture to judge by them, he would have been a speculative individual who would have given a five pound note for the worldly wealth of the trio. Yet, had you taken so much trouble, you might have followed Mr. Blenkins and have seen him picked up by a smart private hansom at the corner of Leman Street. You might then have gone back to the "Hen and Feathers," and have followed Mr. Brown as far as Osborn Street, and have seen him enter a neat brougham, which was evidently his own private property. Another hansom, also a private one, met Mr. Jones in the same thoroughfare, and an hour later two of the number were in Park Lane, while the third was discussing a bottle of Heidseck in a gorgeous private sitting-room on the second floor of the Langham Hotel.

As he entered his dressing-room on his return to Porchester

House, Simon Carne glanced at his watch. It was exactly twelve o'clock.

"I hope Belton will not be long," he said to himself. "Give him a quarter of an hour to rid himself of the other fellow, and say half an hour to get home. In that case he should be here within the next few minutes."

The thought had scarcely passed through his brain before there was a deferential knock at the door, and next moment Belton, clad in a long great coat, entered the room.

"You're back sooner than I expected," said Carne. "You could not have stayed very long with our friend?"

"I left him soon after you did, sir," said Belton. "He was in a hurry to get home, and as there was nothing more to settle I did not attempt to prevent him. I trust you are satisfied, sir, with the result of our adventure."

"Perfectly satisfied," said Carne. "To-morrow I'll make sure that he's good for the money, and then we'll get to work. In the meantime you had better see about a van and the furniture of which I spoke to you, and also engage a man upon whom you can rely."

"But what about Merford, sir, and the attempt upon Knight of Malta?"

"I'll see about that on Monday. I have promised Bent to spend the night there."

"You'll excuse my saying so, sir, I hope," said Belton, as he poured out his master's hot water and laid his dressing-gown upon the back of a chair, ready for him to put on, "but it's a terrible risky business. If we don't bring it off, there'll be such a noise in England as has never been heard before. You might murder the Prime Minister, I believe, and it wouldn't count for so much with the people generally as an attempt to steal the Derby favourite."

"But we shall not fail," said Carne confidently. "By this time you ought to know me better than to suppose that. No, no, never fear, Belton; I've got all my plans cut and dried, and even if we fail to get possession of Vulcanite, the odds are a thousand to one against our being suspected of any complicity in the matter. Now you can go to bed. Good-night."

"Good-night, sir," said Belton respectfully, and left the room.

It was one of Simon Carne's peculiarities always to fulfil his engagements in spite of any inconvenience they might cause himself. Accordingly the four o'clock train from Waterloo, on the Monday following the meeting at the Music Hall just narrated, carried him to Merford in pursuance of the promise he had given his trainer.

Reaching the little wayside station on the edge of the Downs, he alighted, to find himself welcomed by his trainer, who lifted his hat respectfully, and wished him good afternoon.

During the drive, Carne spoke of the impending race, and among other things of a letter he had that morning received, warning him of an attempt that would probably be made to obtain possession of his horse. The trainer laughed good humouredly.

"Bless you, sir," he said, "that's nothing. You should just see some of the letters I've got pasted into my scrap book. Most of 'em comes a week or fortnight before a big race. Some of 'em warns me that if I don't prevent the horse from starting, I'm as good as a dead man; others ask me what price I will take to let him finish outside the first three; while more still tell me that if I don't put 'im out of the way altogether, I'll find my house and my wife and family flying up to the clouds under a full charge of dynamite within three days of the race being run. Don't you pay any attention to the letters you receive. I'll look after the horse, and you may be very sure I'll take good care that nothing happens to him."

"I know that, of course," said Carne, "but I thought I'd tell you. You see, I'm only a novice at racing, and perhaps I place more importance just now upon a threat of that kind than I shall do a couple of years hence."

"Of course," replied the trainer. "I understand exactly how you feel, sir. It's quite natural. And now here we are, with the missis standing on the steps to help me give you a hearty welcome."

They drove up to the door, and when Carne had alighted he was received by the trainer's wife as her lord and master had predicted. His bedroom he discovered, on being conducted to it to prepare for dinner, was at the back of the house, over-looking the stableyard, and possessed a lovely view, extending across the gardens and village towards where the Downs ended and the woods of Herberford began.

"A pretty room," he said to Belton, as the latter laid out his things upon the bed, "and very convenient for our purpose. Have you discovered where you are located?"

"Next door, sir."

"I am glad of that; and what room is beneath us?"

"The kitchen and pantry, sir. With the exception of one at the top of the house, there are no other bedrooms on this side."

"That is excellent news. Now get me ready as soon as you can."

During dinner that evening Simon Carne made himself as pleasant as possible to his host and hostess. So affable, indeed, was he that when they retired to rest they confessed to each other that they had never entertained a more charming guest. It was arranged that he should be called at five o'clock on the morning following, in order that he might accompany the trainer to the Downs to see his horse at his exercise.

It was close upon eleven o'clock when he dismissed his valet and threw himself upon his bed with a novel. For upwards of two hours he amused himself with his book; then he rose and dressed himself in the rough suit which his man had put out for him. Having done so, he took a strong rope ladder from his bag, blew out his light, and opened his window. To attach the hooks at the end of the ropes to the inside of the window sill, and to throw the rest outside was the work of a moment. Then, having ascertained that his door was securely locked, he crawled out and descended to the ground. Once there, he waited until he saw Belton's light disappear, and heard his win-dow softly open. Next moment a small black bag was lowered, and following it, by means of another ladder, came the servant himself.

"There is no time to be lost," said Carne, as soon as they were together. "You must set to work on the big gates, while I do the other business. The men are all asleep; nevertheless, be careful that you make no noise."

Having given his instructions, he left his servant and made his way across the yard towards the box where Knight of Malta was confined. When he reached it he unfastened the bag he had brought with him, and took from it a brace and a peculiar shaped bit, resembling a pair of compasses. Uniting these, he oiled the points and applied them to the door, a little above the lock. What he desired to do did not occupy him for more than a minute.

Then he went quietly along the yard to the further boundary, where he had that afternoon noticed a short ladder. By means of this he mounted to the top of the wall, then lifted it up after him and lowered it on the other side, still without making any noise. Instead of dismounting by it, however, he seated himself for a moment astride of it, while he drew on a pair of clumsy boots he had brought with him, suspended round his neck. Then, having chosen his place, he jumped. His weight caused him to leave a good mark on the soft ground on the other side.

He then walked heavily for perhaps fifty yards, until he reached the high road. Here he divested himself of the boots, put on his list slippers once more, and returned as speedily as possible to the ladder, which he mounted and drew up after him. Having descended on the other side, he left it standing against the wall, and hastened across the yard towards the gates, where he found Belton just finishing the work he had set him to do.

With the aid of a brace and bit similar to that used by Carne upon the stable door, the lock had been entirely removed and the gate stood open. Belton was evidently satisfied with his work; Carne, however, was not so pleased. He picked up the circle of wood and showed it to his servant. Then, taking the bit, he inserted the screw on the reverse side and gave it two or three turns.

"You might have ruined everything," he whispered, "by omitting that. The first carpenter who looked at it would be able to tell that the work was done from the inside. But, thank goodness, I know a trick that will set that right. Now then, give me the pads, and I'll drop them by the door. Then we can return to our rooms."

Four large blanket pads were handed to him, and he went quietly across and dropped them by the stable door. After that he rejoined Belton, and they made their way, with the assistance of the ladders, back to their own rooms once more.

Half an hour later Carne was wrapped in a sweet slumber from which he did not wake until he was aroused by a tapping at his chamber door. It was the trainer.

"Mr. Carne," cried Bent, in what were plainly agitated tones, "if you could make it convenient I should be glad to speak to you as soon as possible."

In something under twenty minutes he was dressed and downstairs. He found the trainer awaiting him in the hall, wearing a very serious face.

"If you will stroll with me as far as the yard, I should like to show you something," he said.

Carne accordingly took up his hat and followed him out of the house.

"You look unusually serious," said the latter, as they crossed the garden.

"An attempt has been made to get possession of your horse."

Carne stopped short in his walk and faced the other.

"What did I tell you yesterday?" he remarked. "I was certain that that letter was more than an idle warning. But how do you know that an attempt *has* been made?"

"Come, sir, and see for yourself," said Bent. "I am sorry to say there is no gainsaying the fact."

A moment later they had reached the entrance to the stable-yard.

"See, sir," said Bent, pointing to a circular hole which now existed where previously the lock had been. "The rascals cut out the lock, and thus gained an entry to the yard."

He picked up the round piece of wood with the lock still attached to it, and showed it to his employer.

"One thing is very certain, the man who cut this hole is a master of his trade, and is also the possessor of fine implements."

"So it would appear," said Carne grimly. "Now what else is there for me to hear? Is the horse much hurt?"

"Not a bit the worse, sir," answered Bent. "They didn't get in at him, you see. Something must have frightened them before they could complete their task. Step this way, sir, if you please, and examine the door of the box for yourself. I have given strict orders that nothing shall be touched until you have seen it."

They crossed the yard together, and approached the box in question. On the woodwork the commencement of a circle similar to that which had been completed on the yard gates could be plainly distinguished, while on the ground below lay four curious shaped pads, one of which Carne picked up.

"What on earth are these things," he asked innocently enough.

"Their use is easily explained, sir," answered the trainer. "They are intended for tying over the horse's feet, so that when he is led out of his box his plates may make no noise upon the stones. I'd like to have been behind 'em with a whip when they got him out, that's all. The double-dyed rascals to try such a trick upon a horse in my charge!"

"I can understand your indignation," said Carne. "It seems to me we have had a narrow escape."

"Narrow escape, or no narrow escape, I'd have had 'em safely locked up in Merford Police Station by this time," replied Bent vindictively. "And now, sir, let me show you how they got out. As far as I can see they must have imagined they heard somebody coming from the house, otherwise they would have left by the gates instead of by this ladder."

He pointed to the ladder, which was still standing where Carne had placed it, and then led him by a side door round to the other side of the wall. Here he pointed to some heavy foot-marks upon the turf. Carne examined them closely.

"If the size of his foot is any criterion of his build," he said, "he must have been a precious big fellow. Let me see how mine compares with it."

He placed his neat shoe in one of the imprints before him, and smiled as he noticed how the other overlapped it.

They then made their way to the box, where they found the animal at his breakfast. He lifted his head and glanced round at them, bit at the iron of the manger, and then gave a little playful kick with one of his hind legs.

"He doesn't seem any the worse for his adventure," said Carne, as the trainer went up to him and ran his hand over his legs.

"Not a bit," answered the other. "He's a wonderfully even-tempered horse, and it takes a lot to put him out. If his nerves had been at all upset he wouldn't have licked up his food as clean as he has done."

Having given another look at him, they left him in charge of his lad, and returned to the house.

The gallop after breakfast confirmed their conclusion that there was nothing the matter, and Simon Carne returned to town ostensibly comforted by Bent's solemn assurance to that effect. That afternoon Lord Calingforth, the owner of Vulcanite, called upon him. They had met repeatedly, and consequently were on the most intimate terms.

"Good afternoon, Carne," he said as he entered the room. "I have come to condole with you upon your misfortune, and to offer you my warmest sympathy."

"Why, what on earth has happened?" asked Carne, as he offered his visitor a cigar.

"God bless my soul, my dear fellow! Haven't you seen the afternoon's paper? Why, it reports the startling news that your stables were broken into last night, and that my rival, Knight of Malta, was missing this morning."

Carne laughed.

"I wonder what they'll say next," he said quietly. "But don't let me appear to deceive you. It is perfectly true that the stables were broken into last night, but the thieves were disturbed, and decamped just as they were forcing the lock of The Knight's box."

"In that case I congratulate you. What rascally inventions some of these sporting papers do get hold of to be sure. I'm indeed glad to hear that it is not true. The race would have lost half its interest if your horse were out of it. By the way, I suppose you are still as confident as ever?"

"Would you like to test it?"

"Very much, if you feel inclined for a bet."

"Then I'll have a level thousand pounds with you that my

horse beats yours. Both to start or the wager is off. Do you agree?"

"With pleasure. I'll make a note of it."

The noble Earl jotted the bet down in his book, and then changed the subject by inquiring whether Carne had ever had any transactions with his next door neighbour, Klimo.

"Only on one occasion," the other replied. "I consulted him on behalf of the Duke of Wiltshire at the time his wife's diamonds were stolen. To tell the truth, I was half thinking of calling him in to see if he could find the fellow who broke into the stables last night, but on second thoughts I determined not to do so. I did not want to make any more fuss about it than I could help. But what makes you ask about Klimo?"

"Well, to put the matter in a nutshell, there has been a good deal of small pilfering down at my trainer's place lately, and I want to get it stopped."

"If I were you I should wait till after the race, and then have him down. If one excites public curiosity just now, one never knows what will happen."

"I think you are right. Anyhow, I'll act on your advice. Now what do you say to coming along to the Rooms with me to see how our horses stand in the market? Your presence there would do more than any number of paper denials towards showing the fallacy of this stupid report. Will you come?"

"With pleasure," said Carne, and in less than five minutes he was sitting beside the noble Earl in his mail phaeton, driving towards the rooms in question.

When he got there, he found Lord Calingforth had stated the case very correctly. The report that Knight of Malta had been stolen had been widely circulated, and Carne discovered that the animal was, for the moment, almost a dead letter in the market. The presence of his owner, however, was sufficient to stay the panic, and when he had snapped up two or three long bets, which a few moments before had been going begging, the horse began steadily to rise towards his old position.

That night, when Belton waited upon his master at bedtime, he found him, if possible, more silent than usual. It was not until his work was well-nigh completed that the other spoke.

"It's a strange thing, Belton," he said, "and you may hardly believe it, but if there were not certain reasons to prevent me from being so magnanimous, I would give this matter up, and let the race be run on its merits. I don't know that I ever took a scheme in hand with a worse grace. However, as it can't be helped, I suppose I must go through with it. Is the van prepared?"

"It is quite ready, sir."

"All the furniture arranged as I directed?"

"It is exactly as you wished, sir. I have attended to it myself."

"And what about the man?"

"I have engaged the young fellow, sir, who assisted me before. I know he's quick, and I can stake my life that he's trustworthy."

"I am glad to hear it. He will have need to be. Now for my arrangements. I shall make the attempt on Friday morning next, that is to say, two days from now. You and the man you have just mentioned will take the van and horses to Market Stopford, travelling by the goods train which, I have discovered, reaches the town between four and five in the morning. As soon as you are out of the station, you will start straight away along the high road towards Exbridge, reaching the village between five and six. I shall meet you in the road alongside the third milestone on the other side, made up for the part I am to play. Do you understand?"

"Perfectly, sir."

"That will do then. I shall go down to the village to-morrow evening, and you will not hear from me again until you meet me at the place I have named. Good-night."

"Good-night, sir."

Now, it is a well-known fact that if you wish to excite the anger of the inhabitants of Exbridge village, and more particularly of any member of the Pitman Training Establishment, you have but to ask for information concerning a certain blind beggar who put in an appearance there towards sunset on the Thursday preceding the Derby of 18—, and you will do so. When that mysterious individual first came in sight he was creeping along the dusty high road that winds across the

Downs from Market Stopford to Beaton Junction, dolorously quavering a ballad that was intended to be, though few would have recognised it, "The Wearing of the Green."

On reaching the stables he tapped along the wall with his stick, until he came to the gate. Then, when he was asked his business by the head lad, who had been called up by one of the stable boys, he stated that he was starving, and, with peculiar arts of his own, induced them to provide him with a meal. For upwards of an hour he remained talking with the lads, and then wended his way down the hill towards the village, where he further managed to induce the rector to permit him to occupy one of his outhouses for the night.

After tea he went out and sat on the green, but towards eight o'clock he crossed the stream at the ford, and made his way up to a little copse, which ornamented a slight eminence, on the opposite side of the village to that upon which the training stables were situated.

How he found his way, considering his infirmity, it is difficult to say, but that he did find it was proved by his presence there. It might also have been noticed that when he was once under cover of the bushes, he gave up tapping the earth with his stick, and walked straight enough, and without apparent hesitation, to the stump of a tree, upon which he seated himself.

For some time he enjoyed the beauty of the evening undisturbed by the presence of any other human being. Then he heard a step behind him, and next moment a smart-looking stable lad parted the bushes and came into view.

"Hullo," said the new-comer. "So you managed to get here first?"

"So I have," said the old rascal, "and it's wonderful when you come to think of it, considering my age, and what a poor old blind chap I be. But I'm glad to find ye've managed to get away, my lad. Now what have ye got to say for yourself?"

"I don't know that I've got anything to say," replied the boy. "But this much is certain, what you want can't be done."

"And a fine young cockerel you are to be sure, to crow so

loud that it can't be done," said the old fellow, with an evil chuckle. "How do you know it can't?"

"Because I don't see my way," replied the other. "It's too dangerous by a long sight. Why, if the Guv'nor was to get wind of what you want me to do, England itself wouldn't be big enough to hold us both. You don't know 'im as well as I do."

"I know him well enough for all practical purposes," replied the beggar. "Now, if you've got any more objections to raise, be quick about it. If you haven't, then I'll talk to you. You haven't? Very good then. Now, just hold your jaw, open your ears, and listen to what I've got to say. What time do you go to exercise to-morrow morning?"

"Nine o'clock."

"Very good then. You go down on to the Downs, and the Boss sends you off with Vulcanite for a canter. What do you do? Why, you go steadily enough as long as he can see you, but directly you're round on the other side of the hill you stick in your heels, and nip into the wood that runs along on your right hand, just as if your horse was bolting with you. Once in there, you go through for half a mile until you come to the stream, ford that, and then cut into the next wood, riding as if the devil himself were after you, until you reach the path above Hangman's Hollow. Do you know the place?"

"I reckon I ought to."

"Well, then, you just make tracks for it. When you get there you'll find me waiting for you. After that I'll take over command, and get both you and the horse out of England in such a way that nobody will ever suspect. Then there'll be five hundred pounds for your trouble, a safe passage with the horse to South America, and another five hundred the day the nag is set ashore. There's not as much risk as you could take between your finger and thumb, and a lad with a spirit like yours could make a fortune with a thousand pounds on the other side. What have you to say now?"

"It's all very well," replied the lad, "but how am I to know that you'll play straight with me?"

"What do you take me for?" said the beggar indignantly, at

the same time putting his hand in his coat pocket and producing what looked like a crumpled piece of paper. "If you doubt me, there's something that may help to convince you. But don't go showing it around to-night, or you'll be giving yourself away, and that'll mean the Stone Jug for you, and 'Amen' to all your hopes of a fortune. You'll do as I wish now, I suppose?"

"I'll do it," said the lad sullenly, as he crumpled the banknote up and put it in his pocket. "But now I must be off. Since there's been this fuss about Knight of Malta, the Guv'nor has us all in before eight o'clock, and keeps the horse under lock and key, with the head lad sleeping in the box with him."

"Well, good-night to you, and don't you forget about to-morrow morning; niggle the horse about a bit just to make him impatient like, and drop a hint that he's a bit fresh. That will make his bolting look more feasible. Don't leave the track while there's any one near you, but, as soon as you do, ride like thunder to the place I told you of. I'll see that they're put off the scent as to the way you've gone."

"All right," said the lad. "I don't like it, but I suppose I'm in too deep now to draw back. Good-night."

"Good-night, and good luck to you."

Once he had got rid of the youth, Carne (for it was he) returned by another route to the rector's out-building, where he laid himself down on the straw, and was soon fast asleep. His slumbers lasted till nearly daybreak, when he rose and made his way across country to the small copse above Hangman's Hollow, on the road from Exbridge to Beaton Junction. Here he discovered a large van drawn up, apparently laden with furniture both inside and out. The horses were feeding beneath a tree, and a couple of men were eating their breakfast beside them. On seeing Carne, the taller of the pair—a respectable-looking workman, with a big brown beard—rose and touched his hat. The other looked with astonishment at the disreputable beggar standing before them.

"So you arrived here safely," said Carne. "If anything you're a little before your time. Boil me a cup of tea, and give me something to eat as quickly as possible, for I am nearly famished. When you have done that, get out the clothes I told you to bring with you, and let me change into them. It wouldn't do for any of the people from the village back yonder to be able to say afterwards that they saw me talking with you in this rig out."

As soon as his hunger was appeased he disappeared into the wood, and dressed himself in his new attire. Another suit of clothes, and an apron such as might be worn by a furniture remover's foreman, a grey wig, a short grey beard and moustache, and a bowler hat, changed his identity completely; indeed, when his rags had been hidden in the hollow of a tree, it would have been a difficult matter to have traced any resemblance between the respectable-looking workman eating his breakfast and the disreputable beggar of half an hour before.

It was close upon nine o'clock by this time, and as soon as he realized this Carne gave the order to put the horses to. This done, they turned their attention to the back of the van, and then a strange thing became apparent. Though to all appearances, viewed from the open doors at the end, the inside of this giant receptacle was filled to its utmost holding capacity with chests of drawers, chairs, bedsteads, carpets, and other articles of household furniture, yet by pulling a pair of handles it was possible for two men easily to withdraw what looked like half the contents of the van.

The poorest observer would then have noticed that in almost every particular these articles were dummies, affixed to a screen, capable of being removed at a moment's notice. The remainder of the van was fitted after the fashion of a stable, with a manger at the end and a pair of slings dependent from the roof.

The nervous tension produced by the waiting soon became almost more than the men could bear. Minute after minute went slowly by, and still the eagerly expected horse did not put in an appearance. Then Belton, whom Carne had placed on the look-out, came flying towards them with the report that he could hear a sound of galloping hoofs in the wood. A few seconds later the noise could be plainly heard at the van, and almost before they had time to comment upon it, a magnificent thoroughbred, ridden by the stable boy who had talked to the blind beggar on the previous evening, dashed into view, and pulled up beside the van.

"Jump off," cried Carne, catching at the horse's head, "and remove the saddle. Now be quick with those cloths; we must rub him down or he'll catch cold."

When the horse was comparatively dry he was led into the van, which was to be his stable for the next few hours, and, in spite of his protests, slung in such a fashion that his feet did not touch the floor. This business completed, Carne bade the frightened boy get in with him, and take care that he did not, on any account, neigh.

After that the mask of furniture was replaced, and the doors closed and locked. The men mounted to their places on the box and roof, and the van continued its journey along the high road towards the Junction. But satisfactory as their attempt had so far proved, the danger was by no means over. Scarcely had they proceeded three miles on their way before Carne distinguished the sound of hoofs upon the road behind him. A moment later a young man, mounted on a well-bred horse, came into view, rode up alongside, and signalled to the driver to stop.

"What's the matter?" inquired the latter, as he brought his horses to a standstill. "Have we dropped anything?"

"Have you seen anything of a boy on a horse?" asked the man, who was so much out of breath that he could scarcely get his words out.

"What sort of a boy, and what sort of a horse?" asked the man on the van.

"A youngish boy," was the reply, "seven stone weight, with sandy hair, on a thoroughbred."

"No: we ain't seen no boy with sandy 'air, ridin' of a thoroughbred 'orse seven stone weight," said Carne. "What's 'e been an' done?"

"The horse has bolted with him off the Downs, back yonder," answered the man. "The Guv'nor has sent us out in all directions to look for him."

"Sorry we can't oblige you," said the driver as he prepared to start his team again. "Good day to you."

"Much obliged," said the horseman, and, when he had

turned off into a side road, the van continued its journey till it reached the railway station. A quarter of an hour later it caught the eleven o'clock goods train and set off for the small seaside town of Barworth, on the south coast, where it was shipped on board a steamer which had arrived that morning from London.

Once it was safely transferred from the railway truck to the deck, Carne was accosted by a tall, swarthy individual, who, from his importance, seemed to be both the owner and the skipper of the vessel. They went down into the saloon together, and a few moments later an observer, had one been there, might have seen a cheque for a considerable sum of money change hands.

An hour later the *Jessie Branker* was steaming out to sea, and a military-looking individual, not at all to be compared with the industrious mechanic, who had shipped the furniture van on board the vessel bound for Spain, stood on the platform of the station waiting for the express train to London. On reaching the metropolis he discovered it surging beneath the weight of a great excitement. The streets re-echoed with the raucous cries of the news-vendors:

"The Derby favourite stolen—Vulcanite missing from his stable!"

Next morning an advertisement appeared in every paper of consequence, offering "A reward of Five Hundred Pounds for any information which might lead to the conviction of the person or persons who on the morning of May 28th had stolen, or caused to be stolen, from the Pitman Training Stables, the Derby favourite, Vulcanite, the property of the Right Honourable the Earl of Calingforth."

The week following, Knight of Malta, owned by Simon Carne, Esq., of Porchester House, Park Lane, won the Derby by a neck, in a scene of intense excitement. The Mandarin being second, and The Filibuster third. It is a strange fact that to this day not a member of the racing world has been able to solve the mystery surrounding the disappearance of one of the greatest horses that ever set foot on an English racecourse.

To-day, if Simon Carne thinks of that momentous occasion,

when, amid the shouting crowd of Epsom he led his horse back a winner, he smiles softly to himself, and murmurs beneath his breath:

"Valued at twenty thousand pounds, and beaten in the Derby by a furniture van."

CHAPTER 3

A SERVICE TO THE STATE

It was the day following that upon which Simon Carne, presented by the Earl of Amberley, had made his bow before the Heir Apparent at the second *levée* of the season, that Klimo entered upon one of the most interesting cases which had so far come into his experience. The clock in his consulting room had just struck one when his elderly housekeeper entered, and handed him a card, bearing the name of Mrs. George Jeffreys, 14, Bellamer Street, Bloomsbury. The detective immediately bade his servant admit the visitor, and, almost before he had given the order, the lady in question stood before him.

She was young, not more than twenty-four at most, a frail wisp of a girl, with light brown hair and eyes that spoke for her nationality as plain as any words. She was neatly, but by no means expensively dressed, and showed evident signs of being oppressed by a weight of trouble. Klimo looked at her, and in that glance took in everything. In spite of the fact that he was reputed to possess a heart as hard as any flint, it was noticeable that his voice, when he spoke to her, was not as gruff as that in which he usually addressed his visitors.

"Pray sit down," he said, "and tell me in as few words as possible what it is you desire that I should do for you. Speak as clearly as you can, and, if you want my help, don't hesitate to tell me everything."

The girl sat down as ordered, and immediately commenced her tale.

"My name is Eileen Jeffreys," she said. "I am the wife of an English Bank Inspector, and the daughter of Septimus O'Grady, of Chicago, U.S.A."

"I shall remember," replied Klimo. "And how long have you been married?"

"Two years," answered the girl. "Two years next September. My husband and I met in America, and then came to England to settle."

"In saying good-bye to your old home, you left your father behind, I presume?"

"Yes, he preferred to remain in America."

"May I ask his profession?"

"That, I'm afraid, foolish as it may seem to say so, I cannot tell you," answered the girl, with a slightly heightened colour. "His means of earning a living were always kept a secret from me."

"That was rather strange, was it not?" said Klimo. "Had he private resources?"

"None that I ever heard of," replied the girl.

"Did no business men ever come to see him?"

"But very few people came to us at all. We had scarcely any friends."

"Of what nationality were the friends who *did* come?"

"Mostly Irish, like ourselves," answered Mrs. Jeffreys.

"Was there ever any quarrel between your father and your husband, prior to your leaving America?"

"Never any downright quarrel," said the girl. "But I am sorry to say they were not always the best of friends. In those days my father was a very difficult man to get on with."

"Indeed?" said Klimo. "Now, perhaps you had better proceed with your story."

"To do that, I must explain that at the end of January of this present year, my father, who was then in Chicago, sent us a cablegram to say he was leaving for England that very day, and, that upon his arrival in England, if we had no objection, he would like to take up his residence with us. He was to sail from New York on the Saturday following, and, as you know, the passage takes six days or thereabouts. Arriving in England he came to London and put up at our house in Bellamer Street, Bloomsbury. That was during the first week in February last, and off and on he has been living with us ever since."

"Have you any idea what brought him to England?"

"Not the least," she answered deliberately, after a few seconds' pause, which Klimo did not fail to notice.

"Did he do business with any one that you are aware of?"

"I cannot say. On several occasions he went away for a week at a time into the Midlands, but what took him there I have no possible idea. On the last occasion he left us on the fifteenth of last month, and returned on the ninth of this, the same day that my husband was called away to Marseilles on important banking business. It was easy to see that he was not well. He was feverish, and within a short time of my getting him to bed began to wander in his mind, declaring over and over again that he bitterly repented some action he had taken, and that if he could once consider himself safe again would be quit of the whole thing for ever.

"For close upon a fortnight I continued to nurse him, until he was so far recovered as to recognise me once more. The day that he did so I took in at the door this cablegram, from which I may perhaps date the business that has brought me to you."

She took a paper from her pocket and handed it to Klimo, who glanced at it, examined the post-mark and the date, and then placed it upon the desk before him. It was from Chicago, and ran as follows:—

O'Grady,
   13, Bellamer Street, London, England.
Why no answer? Reply chances of doing business.

NERO.

"Of course, it was impossible for me to tell what this meant. I was not in my father's confidence, and I had no notion who his mysterious correspondent might be. But as the doctor had distinctly stated that to allow him to consider any business at all would bring on a relapse and probably kill him, I placed the message in a drawer, and determined to let it remain there until he should be well enough to attend to it without danger to himself. The week following he was not quite so well, and fortunately there was complete silence on the part of his correspondents. Then this second message arrived. As you will see it is also from Chicago and from the same person.

> Reply immediately, or remember consequences. Time presses, if do not realise at present price, market will be lost.
>
> NERO.

"Following my previous line of action, I placed this communication also in the drawer, and determined to let Nero wait for a reply. By doing so, however, I was incurring greater trouble than I dreamt of. Within forty-eight hours I received the following message, and upon that I made up my mind and came off at once to you. What it means I do not know, but that it bodes some ill to my father I feel certain. I had heard of your fame, and as my husband is away from home, my father unable to protect himself, and I am without friends at all in England, I thought the wisest course I could pursue would be to consult you."

"Let me look at the last cablegram," said Klimo, putting his hand from the box, and taking the slip of paper.

The first and second messages were simplicity itself; this, however, was a complete enigma. It was worded as follows:—

> Uneasy—Alpha—Omega—Nineteen—Twelve—to-day—five—lacs—arrange—seventy—eight—Brazils—one—twenty—nine.
>
> NERO.

Klimo read it through, and the girl noticed that he shook his head over it.

"My dear young lady," he said, "I am afraid that it would be safer for you not to tell me any further, for I fear it is not in my power to help you."

"You will not help me now that I have told you my miserable position? Then there is nothing before me but despair. Oh, sir, is your decision quite irrevocable? You cannot think how I have counted on your assistance."

"I regret exceedingly that I am compelled to disappoint you," he answered. "But my time is more than occupied as it is, and I could not give your case my attention, even if I would."

His decision had been too much for her fortitude, and before he could prevent it, her head was down upon her hands and she had begun to weep bitterly. He attempted to comfort her, but in vain; and when she left him, tears were still coursing down her cheeks. It was not until she had been gone about ten minutes, and he had informed his housekeeper that he would see no more clients that day, that he discovered that she had left her precious cablegrams behind her.

Actuated by a feeling of curiosity, he sat down again and spread the three cablegrams out upon his writing-table. The first two, as I have said, required no consideration, they spoke for themselves, but the third baffled him completely. Who was this Septimus O'Grady who lived in Chicago, and whose associates spent their time discussing the wrongs of Ireland? How was it that, being a man innocent of private means, he engaged in no business?

Then another question called for consideration. If he had no business, what brought him to London and took him so repeatedly into the Midlands? These riddles he set aside for the present, and began to pick the last cablegram to pieces. That its author was not easy in his mind when he wrote it was quite certain.

Then who and what were the Alpha and Omega mentioned? What connection had they with Nero; also what did nineteen and twelve mean when coupled with To-day? Further, why should five lacs arrange seventy-eight Brazils? And what possible sense could be made out of the numbers one—twenty—and nine? He read the message from beginning to end again, after that from the end to the beginning, and, like a good many other men in a similar position, because he could not understand it, found himself taking a greater interest in it. This feeling had not left him when he had put off disguise as Klimo and was Simon Carne once more.

While he was eating his lunch the thought of the lonely Irishman lying ill in a house, where he was without doubt an unwelcome guest, fascinated him strangely, and when he rose from the table he found he was not able to shake off the impression it had given him. That the girl had some notion of her father's business he felt as certain as of his own name, even though she had so strenuously denied the fact. Otherwise why should she have been so frightened by what might have been simply innocent business messages in cypher? That she *was* frightened was as plain as the sun then shining into his room. Despite the fact that he had resolved not to take up the case, he went into his study, and took the cablegrams from the drawer in which he had placed them. Then drawing a sheet of paper towards him, he set to work upon the puzzle.

"The first word requires no explanation," he said as he wrote it down. "For the two next, Alpha and Omega, we will, for the sake of argument, write The Beginning and The End, and as that tells us nothing, we will substitute for them The First and The Last. Now, who or what are The First and The Last? Are they the first and last words of a code, or of a word, or do they refer to two individuals who are the principal folk in some company or conspiracy? If the latter, it is just possible they are the people who are so desperately uneasy. The next two words, however, are too much for me altogether."

Uninteresting as the case had appeared at first sight, he soon discovered that he could think of nothing else. He found himself puzzling over it during an afternoon concert at the Queen's Hall, and he even thought of it while calling upon the wife of the Prime Minister afterwards. As he drove in the Park before dinner, the wheels of his carriage seemed to be saying "Alpha and Omega, nineteen, twelve" over and over again with pitiless reiteration, and by the time he reached home once more he would gladly have paid a ten-pound note for a feasible solution of the enigma, if only to get its weight off his mind.

While waiting for dinner he took pen and paper and wrote the message out again, this time in half a dozen different ways. But the effect was the same, none of them afforded him any clue. He then took the second letter of each word, after that the third, then the fourth, and so on until he had exhausted them. The result in each case was absolute gibberish, and he felt that he was no nearer understanding it than when Mrs. Jeffreys had handed it to him nearly eight hours before.

During the night he dreamt about it, and when he woke in the morning its weight was still upon his mind. "Nineteen—twelve," it is true had left him, but he was no better off for the reason that "Seventy-eight Brazils" had taken its place. When he got out of bed he tried it again. But at the end of half an hour his patience was exhausted.

"Confound the thing," he said, as he threw the paper from him, and seated himself in a chair before his looking-glass in order that his confidential valet, Belton, might shave him. "I'll think no more of it. Mrs. Jeffreys must solve the mystery for herself. It has worried me too much already."

He laid his head back upon the rest and allowed his valet to run the soap brush over his chin. But, however much he might desire it his Old Man of the Sea was not to be discarded so easily; the word "Brazils" seemed to be printed in letters of fire upon the ceiling. As the razor glided over his cheek he thought of the various constructions to be placed upon the word—The Country—Stocks—and even nuts—Brazil nuts, Spanish nuts, Barcelona nuts, walnuts, cob nuts—and then, as if to make the nightmare more complete, no less a thing than Nuttall's Dictionary. The smile the last suggestion caused him came within an ace of leaving its mark upon his cheek. He signed to the man to stay his hand.

"Egad!" he cried, "who knows but this may be the solution of the mystery? Go down to the study, Belton, and bring me Nuttall's Dictionary."

He waited with one side of his face still soaped until his valet returned, bringing with him the desired volume. Having received it he placed it upon the table and took up the telegram.

"Seventy—eight Brazils," it said, "one—twenty—nine."

Accordingly he chose the seventieth page, and ran his fingers down the first column. The letter was B, but the eighth word proved useless. He thereupon turned to the seventy-eighth page, and in the first column discovered the word *Bomb*. In a second the whole aspect of the case changed, and he became all eagerness and excitement. The last words on the telegram were "one-twenty-nine," yet it was plain that there were barely a hundred upon the page. The only explanation, therefore, was that the word "One" distinguished the column, and the "twenty-nine" referred to the number of the word in it.

Almost trembling with eagerness he began to count. Surely enough the twenty-ninth word *was* Bomb. The coincidence was, to say the least of it, extraordinary. But presuming that it was correct, the rest of the message was simplicity itself. He turned the telegram over, and upon the back transcribed the communication as he imagined it should be read. When he had finished, it ran as follows:

> Owing to O'Grady's silence, the Society in Chicago is growing uneasy. Two men, who are the first and last, or, in other words, the principal members, are going to do something (Nineteen-twelve) to-day with fifty thousand somethings, so arrange about the bombs.

Having got so far, all that remained to be done was to find out to what "nineteen-twelve" referred. He turned to the dictionary again, and looked for the twelfth word upon the nineteenth page. This proved to be "Alkahest," which told him nothing. So he reversed the proceedings and looked for the nineteenth word upon the twelfth page; but this proved even less satisfactory than before. However much the dictionary might have helped him hitherto, it was plainly useless now. He thought and thought, but without success. He turned up the almanac, but the dates did not fit in.

He then wrote the letters of the alphabet upon a sheet of paper, and against each placed its equivalent number. The nineteenth letter was S, the twelfth L. Did they represent two words, or were they the first and the last letters of a word? In that case, what could it be. The only three he could think of were *soil*, *sell*, and *sail*. The two first were hopeless, but the last seemed better. But how would that fit in? He took up his pen and tried it.

> Owing to O'Grady's silence, the Society in Chicago is growing uneasy. Two men, who are the first and last, or, in other words,

the principal members, sail to-day with fifty thousand some-
things, probably pounds or dollars, so prepare bombs.

NERO.

He felt convinced that he had hit it at last. Either it was a
very extraordinary coincidence, or he had discovered the
answer to the riddle. If his solution were correct, one thing
was certain, he had got in his hands, quite by chance, a clue to
one of the biggest Fenian conspiracies ever yet brought to light.
He remembered that at that moment London contained half
the crowned heads, or their representatives, of Europe. What
better occasion could the enemies of law and order desire for
striking a blow at the Government and society in general?
What was he to do?

To communicate with the police and thus allow himself to
be drawn into the affair, would be an act of the maddest folly;
should he therefore drop the whole thing, as he had at first
proposed, or should he take the matter into his own hands,
help Mrs. Jeffreys in her trouble by shipping her father out of
harm's way, outwit the Fenians, and appropriate the fifty thousand pounds mentioned in the cablegram himself?

The last idea was distinctly a good one. But, before it could
be done, he felt he must be certain of his facts. Was the fifty
thousand referred to money, or was it something else? If the
former, was it pounds or was it dollars? There was a vast difference, but in either case, if only he could hit on a safe scheme,
he would be well repaid for whatever risk he might run. He
decided to see Mrs. Jeffreys without loss of time. Accordingly,
after breakfast, he sent her a note asking her to call upon him,
without fail, at twelve o'clock.

Punctuality is not generally considered a virtue possessed by
the sex of which Mrs. Jeffreys was so unfortunate a member,
but the clock upon Klimo's mantelpiece had scarcely struck
the hour before she put in an appearance. He immediately
bade her be seated.

"Mrs. Jeffreys," he began with a severely judicial air, "it is
with much regret I find that while seeking my advice yesterday
you were all the time deceiving me. How was it that you failed

to tell me that your father was connected with a Fenian Society, whose one aim and object is to destroy law and order in this country?"

The question evidently took the girl by surprise. She became deathly pale, and for a moment Klimo thought she was going to faint. With a marvellous exhibition of will, however, she pulled herself together and faced her accuser.

"You have no right to say such a thing," she began. "My father is——"

"Pardon me," he answered quietly, "but I am in the possession of information which enables me to understand exactly *what* he is. If you answer me correctly it is probable that after all I will take your case up, and will help you to save your father's life, but if you decline to do so, ill as he is, he will be arrested within twenty-four hours, and then nothing on earth can save him from condign punishment. Which do you prefer?"

"I will tell you everything," she said quickly. "I ought to have done so at first, but you can understand why I shrank from it. My father has for a long time past been ashamed of the part he has been playing, but he could not help himself. He was too valuable to them, and they would not let him slip. They drove him on and on, and it was his remorse and anxiety that broke him down at last."

"I think you have chosen the better course in telling me this. I will ask my questions, and you can answer them. To begin with, where are the headquarters of the Society?"

"In Chicago."

"I thought as much. And is it possible for you to tell me the names of the two principal members?"

"There are many members, and I don't know that one *is* greater than another."

"But there must be some who are more important than others. For instance, the pair referred to in this telegram as Alpha and Omega?"

"I can only think," she answered, after a moment's thought, "that they must be the two men who came oftenest to our house, Messrs. Maguire and Rooney."

"Can you describe them, or, better still, have you their photographs?"

"I have a photograph of Mr. Rooney. It was taken last year."

"You must send it to me as soon as you get home," he said; "and now give me as close a description as possible of the other person to whom you refer, Mr. Maguire."

Mrs. Jeffreys considered for a few moments before she answered.

"He is tall, standing fully six feet, I should think," she said at last, "with red hair and watery blue eyes, in the left of which there is a slight cast. He is broad shouldered and, in spite of his long residence in America, speaks with a decided brogue. I know them for desperate men, and if they come over to England may God help us all. Mr. Klimo, you don't think the police will take my father?"

"Not if you implicitly obey my instructions," he answered.

Klimo thought for a few seconds, and then continued: "If you wish me to undertake this business, which I need hardly tell you is out of my usual line, you will now go home and send me the photograph you spoke of a few moments since. After that you will take no sort of action until you hear from me again. For certain reasons of my own I shall take this matter up, and will do my utmost to save your father. One word of advice first, say nothing to anybody, but pack your father's boxes and be prepared to get him out of England, if necessary, at a moment's notice."

The girl rose and made as if she would leave the room, but instead of doing so she stood irresolute. For a few moments she said nothing, but fumbled with the handle of her parasol and breathed heavily. Then the pluck which had so far sustained her gave way entirely, and she fell back on her chair crying as if her heart would break. Klimo instantly left his box and went round to her. He made a figure queer enough to please any one, in his old-fashioned clothes, his skull cap, his long grey hair reaching almost to his shoulders, and with his smoked glass spectacles perched upon his nose.

"Why cry, my dear young lady?" said Klimo. "Have I not promised to do my best for you? Let us, however, understand each other thoroughly. If there is anything you are keeping back you must tell me. By not speaking out you are imperilling your own and your father's safety."

"I know that you must think that I am endeavouring to deceive you," she said; "but I am so terribly afraid of committing myself that I hardly know what to tell and what not to tell. I have come to you, having no friends in the whole world save my husband, who is in Marseilles, and my father, who, as I have said, is lying dangerously ill in our house.

"Of course I know what my father has been. Surely you cannot suppose that a grown up girl like myself could be so dense as not to guess why few save Irishmen visited our house, and why at times there were men staying with us for weeks at a time, who lived in the back rooms and never went outside our front door, and who, when they did take their departure, sneaked out in the dead of night.

"I remember a time in the fall of the last year that I was at home, when there were more meetings than ever, and when these men, Maguire and Rooney, almost lived with us. They and my father were occupied day and night in a room at the top of the house, and then, in the January following, Maguire came to England. Three weeks later the papers were full of a terrible dynamite explosion in London, in which forty innocent people lost their lives. Mr. Klimo, you must imagine for yourself the terror and shame that seized me, particularly when I remembered that my father was a companion of the men who had been concerned in it.

"Now my father repents, and they are edging him on to some fresh outrage. I cannot tell you what it is, but I know this, that if Maguire and Rooney are coming to England, something awful is about to happen, and if they distrust him, and there is any chance of any one getting into trouble, my father will be made the scapegoat.

"To run away from them would be to court certain death. They have agents in almost every European city, and, unless we could get right away to the other side of the world, they would be certain to catch us. Besides, my father is too ill to travel. The doctors say he must not be disturbed under any pretence whatever."

"Well, well!" said Kilmo, "leave the matter to me, and I will see what can be done. Send me the photograph you spoke of, and let me know instantly if there are any further developments."

"Do you mean that after all I can rely upon you helping me?"

"If you are brave," he answered, "not without. Now, one last question, and then you must be off. I see in the last telegram, mention made of fifty lacs; I presume that means money?"

"A lac is their term for a thousand pounds," she answered without hesitation.

"That will do," said Klimo. "Now go home and don't worry yourself more than you can help. Above all, don't let any one suspect that I have any interest in the case. Upon your doing that will in a great measure depend your safety."

She promised to obey him in this particular as in the others, and then took her departure.

When Klimo had passed into the adjoining house, he bade his valet accompany him to his study.

"Belton," he said, as he seated himself in a comfortable chair before his writing table, "I have this morning agreed to undertake what promises to be one of the most dangerous, and at the same time most interesting, cases that has yet come under my notice. A young lady, the wife of a respectable Bank Inspector, has been twice to see me lately with a very sad story. Her father, it would appear, is an Irish American, with the usual prejudice against this country. He has been for some time a member of a Fenian Society, possibly one of their most active workers. In January last the executive sent him to this country to arrange for an exhibition of their powers.

"Since arriving here the father has been seized with remorse, and the mental strain and fear thus entailed have made him seriously ill. For weeks he has been lying at death's door in his daughter's house. Hearing nothing from him the Society has telegraphed again and again, but without result. In consequence, two of the chief and most dangerous members are coming over here with fifty thousand pounds at their disposal, to look after their erring brother, to take over the management of affairs, and to commence the slaughter as per arrangement.

"Now as a peaceable citizen of the City of London, and a humble servant of Her Majesty the Queen, it is manifestly my duty to deliver these rascals into the hands of the police. But to do that would be to implicate the girl's father, and to kill her husband's faith in her family; for it must be remembered he knows nothing of the father's Fenian tendencies. It would also mix me up in a most undesirable matter at a time when I have the best of reasons for desiring to keep quiet.

"Well, the long and the short of the matter is that I have been thinking the question out, and I have arrived at the following conclusion. If I can hit upon a workable scheme I shall play policeman and public benefactor, checkmate the dynamiters, save the girl and her father, and reimburse myself to the extent of fifty thousand pounds. Fifty thousand pounds, Belton, think of that. If it hadn't been for the money I should have had nothing at all to do with it."

"But how will you do it, sir?" asked Belton, who had learnt by experience never to be surprised at anything his master might say or do.

"Well, so far," he answered, "it seems a comparatively easy matter. I see that the last telegram was dispatched on Saturday, May 26th, and says, or purports to say, *'sail to-day.'* In that case, all being well, they should be in Liverpool some time to-morrow, Thursday. So we have a clear day at our disposal in which to prepare a reception for them. To-night I am to have a photograph of one of the men in my possession, and to-morrow I shall send you to Liverpool to meet them. Once you have set eyes on them you must not lose sight of them until you have discovered where they are domiciled in London. After that I will take the matter in hand myself."

"At what hour do you wish me to start for Liverpool, sir?" asked Belton.

"First thing to-morrow morning," his master replied. "In the meantime you must, by hook or crook, obtain a police inspector's, a sergeant's, and two constable's uniforms with belts and helmets complete. Also I shall require three men in whom I can place absolute and implicit confidence. They must be big fellows with plenty of pluck and intelligence, and the clothes you get must fit them so that they shall not look awkward in them. They must also bring plain clothes with them, for I shall want two of them to undertake a journey to Ireland. They will each be paid a hundred pounds for the job, and to ensure their silence afterwards. Do you think you can find me the men without disclosing my connection with the matter?"

"I know exactly where to put my hand upon them, sir," remarked Belton, "and for the sum you mention it's my belief they'd hold their tongues for ever, no matter what pressure was brought to bear upon them."

"Very good. You had better communicate with them at once, and tell them to hold themselves in readiness, for I may want them at any moment. On Friday night I shall probably attempt the job, and they can get back to town when and how they like."

"Very good, sir. I'll see about them this afternoon without fail."

Next morning, Belton left London for Liverpool, with the photograph of the mysterious Rooney in his pocket-book. Carne had spent the afternoon with a fashionable party at Hurlingham, and it was not until he returned to his house that he received the telegram he had instructed his valet to send him. It was short, and to the point.

Friends arrived. Reach Euston nine o'clock.

The station clocks wanted ten minutes of the hour when the hansom containing a certain ascetic looking curate drove into the yard. The clergyman paid his fare, and, having inquired the platform upon which the Liverpool express would arrive, strolled leisurely in that direction. He would have been a clever man who would have recognised in this unsophisticated individual either deformed Simon Carne, of Park Lane, or the famous detective of Belverton Street.

Punctual almost to the moment the train put in an appearance, and drew up beside the platform. A moment later the curate was engulfed in a sea of passengers. A bystander, had he been sufficiently observant to notice such a thing, would have been struck by the eager way in which he looked about him, and also by the way in which his manner changed directly he went forward to greet the person he was expecting.

To all appearances they were both curates, but their social positions must have been widely different if their behaviour to each other could have been taken as any criterion. The new arrival, having greeted his friend, turned to two gentlemen standing beside him, and after thanking them for their company during the journey, wished them a pleasant holiday in England, and bade them good-bye. Then, turning to his friend again, he led him along the platform towards the cab rank.

During the time Belton had been speaking to the two men just referred to, Carne had been studying their faces attentively. One, the taller of the pair, if his red hair and watery blue eyes went for anything, was evidently Maguire, the other was Rooney, the man of the photograph. Both were big, burly fellows, and Carne felt that if it ever came to a fight, they would be just the sort of men to offer a determined resistance.

Arm in arm the curates followed the Americans towards the cab rank. Reaching it, the latter called up a vehicle, placed the bags they carried upon the roof, and took their places inside. The driver had evidently received his instructions, for he drove off without delay. Carne at once called up another cab, into which Belton sprang without ceremony. Carne pointed to the cab just disappearing through the gates ahead.

"Keep that hansom in sight, cabby," he said; "but whatever you do don't pass it."

"All right, sir," said the man, and immediately applied the whip to his horse.

When they turned into Seymour Street, scarcely twenty yards separated the two vehicles, and in this order they proceeded across the Euston Road, by way of Upper Woburn Place and Tavistock Square.

The cab passed through Bloomsbury Square, and turned down one of the thoroughfares leading therefrom, and made its way into a street flanked on either side by tall, gloomy-looking houses. Leaning over the apron, Carne gazed up at the corner house, on which he could just see the plate setting forth the name of the street. What he saw there told him all he wanted to know.

They were in Bellamer Street, and it was plain to him that the men had determined to thrust themselves upon the hapless Mrs. Jeffreys. He immediately poked his umbrella through the shutter, and bade the cabman drive on to the next corner, and then pull up. As soon as the horse came to a standstill, Carne jumped out, and, bidding his companion drive home, crossed the street, and made his way back until he arrived at a spot exactly opposite the house entered by the two men.

His supposition that they intended to domicile themselves there was borne out by the fact that they had taken their luggage inside, and had dismissed their cab. There had been lights in two of the windows when the cab had passed, now a third was added, and this he set down as emanating from the room allotted to the new arrivals.

For upwards of an hour and a half Carne remained standing in the shadow of the opposite houses, watching the Jeffreys' residence. The lights in the lower room had by this time disappeared, and within ten minutes that on the first floor followed suit. Being convinced, in his own mind, that the inmates were safely settled for the night, he left the scene of his vigil, and, walking to the corner of the street, hailed a hansom and was driven home. On reaching No. 1, Belverton Street, he found a letter lying on the hall table addressed to Klimo. It was in a woman's handwriting, and it did not take him long to guess that it was from Mrs. Jeffreys. He opened it and read as follows:

BELLAMER STREET,
Thursday Evening.

DEAR MR. KLIMO,—

I am sending this to you to tell you that my worst suspicions have been realised. The two men whose coming I so dreaded, have arrived, and have taken up their abode with us. For my father's sake I dare not turn them out, and to-night I have heard from my husband to say that he will be home on Saturday next. What is to be done? If something does not happen soon, they will commence their dastardly business in England, and then God help us all. My only hope is in Him and you.

Yours ever gratefully,
EILEEN JEFFREYS.

Carne folded up the letter with a grave face, and then let himself into Porchester House and went to bed to think out his plan of action. Next morning he was up betimes, and by the breakfast hour had made up his mind as to what he was going to do. He had also written and dispatched a note to the girl who was depending so much upon him. In it he told her to come and see him without fail that morning. His meal finished, he went to his dressing-room and attired himself in Klimo's clothes, and shortly after ten o'clock entered the detective's house. Half an hour later Mrs. Jeffreys was ushered into his presence. As he greeted her he noticed that she looked pale and wan. It was evident she had spent a sleepless night.

"Sit down," he said, "and tell me what has happened since last I saw you."

"The most terrible thing of all has happened," she answered, "As I told you in my note, the men have reached England, and are now living in our house. You can imagine what a shock their arrival was to me. I did not know what to do. For my father's sake I could not refuse them admittance, and yet I knew that I had no right to take them in during my husband's absence. Be that as it may, they are there now, and to-morrow night George returns. If he discovers their identity, and suspects their errand, he will hand them over to the police without a second thought, and then we shall be disgraced for ever. Oh, Mr. Klimo, you promised to help me, can you not do so? Heaven knows how badly I need your aid."

"You shall have it. Now listen to my instructions. You will go home and watch these men. During the afternoon they will probably go out, and the instant they do so, you must admit three of my servants and place them in some room where their presence will not be suspected by our enemies. A friend, who will hand you my card, will call later on, and as he will take command, you must do your best to help him in every possible way."

"You need have no fear of my not doing that," she said. "And I will be grateful to you till my dying day."

"Well, we'll see. Now good-bye."

After she had left him, Klimo returned to Porchester House and sent for Belton. He was out, it appeared, but within half an hour he returned and entered his master's presence.

"Have you discovered the bank?" asked Carne.

"Yes, sir, I have," said Belton. "But not till I was walked off my legs. The men are as suspicious as wild rabbits, and they dodged and played about so, that I began to think they'd get away from me altogether. The bank is the 'United Kingdom,' Oxford Street branch."

"That's right. Now what about the uniforms?"

"They're quite ready, sir, helmets, tunics, belts and trousers complete."

"Well then have them packed as I told you yesterday, and ready to proceed to Bellamer Street with the men, the instant we get the information that the folk we are after have stepped outside the house door."

"Very good, sir. And as to yourself?"

"I shall join you at the house at ten o'clock, or thereabouts. We must, if possible, catch them at their supper."

London was half through its pleasures that night, when a tall, military-looking man, muffled in a large cloak, stepped into a hansom outside Porchester House, Park Lane, and drove off in the direction of Oxford Street. Though the business which was taking him out would have presented sufficient dangers to have deterred many men who consider themselves not wanting in pluck, it did not in the least oppress Simon Carne; on the contrary, it seemed to afford him no small amount of satisfaction. He whistled a tune to himself as he drove along the lamplit thoroughfares, and smiled as sweetly as a lover

thinking of his mistress when he reviewed the plot he had so
cunningly contrived.

He felt a glow of virtue as he remembered that he was undertaking the business in order to promote another's happiness,
but at the same time reflected that, if fate were willing to pay
him fifty thousand pounds for his generosity, well, it was so
much the better for him. Reaching Mudie's Library, his coachman drove by way of Hart Street into Bloomsbury Square, and
later on turned into Bellamer Street.

At the corner he stopped his driver and gave him some
instructions in a low voice. Having done so, he walked along
the pavement as far as No. 14, where he came to a standstill.
As on the last occasion that he had surveyed the house, there
were lights in three of the windows, and from this illumi-
nation he argued that his men were at home. Without hesitation he went up the steps and rang the bell. Before he could
have counted fifty it was opened by Mrs. Jeffreys herself, who
looked suspiciously at the person she saw before her. It was
evident that in the tall, well-made man with iron-grey moustache and dark hair, she did not recognise her elderly acquaintance, Klimo, the detective.

"Are you Mrs. Jeffreys?" asked the newcomer, in a low
voice.

"I am," she answered. "Pray, what can I do for you?"

"I was told by a friend to give you this card."

He thereupon handed to her a card on which was written
the one word "Klimo." She glanced at it, and, as if that magic
name were sufficient to settle every doubt, beckoned to him to
follow her. Having softly closed the door she led him down the
passage until she arrived at a door on her right hand. This she
opened and signed to him to enter. It was a room that was half
office half library.

"I am to understand that you come from Mr. Klimo?" she
said, trembling under the intensity of her emotion. "What am
I to do?"

"First be as calm as you can. Then tell me where the men
are with whom I have to deal."

"They are having their supper in the dining-room. They went out soon after luncheon, and only returned an hour ago."

"Very good. Now, if you will conduct me upstairs, I shall be glad to see if your father is well enough to sign a document I have brought with me. Nothing can be done until I have arranged that."

"If you will come with me I will take you to him. But we must go quietly, for the men are so suspicious that they send for me to know the meaning of every sound. I was dreadfully afraid your ring would bring them out into the hall."

Leading the way up the stairs she conducted him to a room on the first floor, the door of which she opened carefully. On entering, Carne found himself in a well-furnished bedroom. A bed stood in the centre of the room, and on this lay a man. In the dim light, for the gas was turned down till it showed scarcely a glimmer, he looked more like a skeleton than a human being. A long white beard lay upon the coverlet, his hair was of the same colour, and the pallor of his skin more than matched both. That he was conscious was shown by the question he addressed to his daughter as they entered.

"What is it, Eileen?" he asked faintly. "Who is this gentleman, and why does he come to see me?"

"He is a friend, father," she answered. "One who has come to save us from these wicked men."

"God bless you, sir," said the invalid, and as he spoke he made as if he would shake him by the hand.

Carne, however, checked him.

"Do not move or speak," he said, "but try and pull yourself together sufficiently to sign this paper."

"What is the document?"

"It is something without which I can take no sort of action. My instructions are to do nothing until you have signed it. You need not be afraid; it will not hurt you. Come, sir, there is no time to be wasted. If these rascals are to be got out of England our scheme must be carried out to-night."

"To do that I will sign anything. I trust your honour for its contents. Give me a pen and ink."

His daughter supported him in her arms, while Carne dipped a pen in the bottle of ink he had brought with him and placed it in the tremulous fingers. Then, the paper being supported on a book, the old man laboriously traced his signature at the place indicated. When he had done so he fell back upon the pillow completely exhausted.

Carne blotted it carefully, then folded the paper up, placed it in his pocket and announced himself ready for work. The clock upon the mantelpiece showed him that it was a quarter to eleven, so that if he intended to act that night he knew he must do so quickly. Bidding the invalid rest happy in the knowledge that his safety was assured, he beckoned the daughter to him.

"Go downstairs," he said in a whisper, "and make sure that the men are still in the dining-room."

She did as he ordered her, and in a few moments returned with the information that they had finished their supper and had announced their intention of going to bed.

"In that case we must hurry," said Carne. "Where are my men concealed?"

"In the room at the end of that passage," was the girl's reply.

"I will go to them. In the meantime you must return to the study downstairs, where we will join you in five minutes' time. Just before we enter the room in which they are sitting, one of my men will ring the front door bell. You must endeavour to make the fellows inside believe that you are trying to prevent us from gaining admittance. We shall arrest you, and then deal with them. Do you understand?"

"Perfectly."

She slipped away, and Carne hastened to the room at the end of the passage. He scratched with his finger nail upon the door, and a second later it was opened by a sergeant of police. On stepping inside he found two constables and an inspector awaiting him.

"Is all prepared, Belton?" he inquired of the latter.

"Quite prepared, sir."

"Then come along, and step as softly as you can."

As he spoke he took from his pocket a couple of papers, and

led the way along the corridor and down the stairs. With infinite care they made their way along the hall until they reached the dining-room door, where Mrs. Jeffreys joined them. Then the street bell rang loudly, and the man who had opened the front door a couple of inches shut it with a bang. Without further hesitation Carne called upon the woman to stand aside, while Belton threw open the dining-room door.

"I tell you, sir, you are mistaken," cried the terrified woman.

"I am the best judge of that," said Carne roughly, and then, turning to Belton, he added: "Let one of your men take charge of this woman."

On hearing them enter, the two men they were in search of had risen from the chairs they had been occupying on either side of the fire, and stood side by side upon the hearth rug, staring at the intruders as if they did not know what to do.

"James Maguire and Patrick Wake Rooney," said Carne, approaching the two men, and presenting the papers he held in his hand, "I have here warrants, and arrest you both on a charge of being concerned in a Fenian plot against the well being of Her Majesty's Government. I should advise you to submit quietly. The house is surrounded, constables are posted at all the doors, and there is not the slightest chance of escape."

The men seemed too thunderstruck to do anything, and submitted quietly to the process of handcuffing. When they had been secured, Carne turned to the inspector and said:

"With regard to the other man who is ill upstairs, Septimus O'Grady, you had better post a man at his door."

"Very good, sir."

Then turning to Messrs. Maguire and Rooney, he said: "I am authorised by Her Majesty's Government to offer you your choice between arrest and appearance at Bow Street, or immediate return to America. Which do you choose? I need not tell you that we have proof enough in our hands to hang the pair of you if necessary. You had better make up your minds as quickly as possible, for I have no time to waste."

The men stared at him in supreme astonishment.

"You will not prosecute us?"

"My instructions are, in the event of your choosing the

latter alternative, to see that you leave the country at once. In fact, I shall conduct you to Kingstown myself to-night, and place you aboard the mail-boat there."

"Well, so far as I can see, it's Hobson's choice," said Maguire. "I'll pay you the compliment of saying that you're smarter than I thought you'd be. How did you come to know we were in England?"

"Because your departure from America was cabled to us more than a week ago. You have been shadowed ever since you set foot ashore. Now passages have been booked for you on board the outgoing boat, and you will sail in her. First, however, it will be necessary for you to sign this paper, pledging yourselves never to set foot in England again."

"And supposing we do not sign it?"

"In that case I shall take you both to Bow Street forthwith, and you will come before the magistrates in the morning. You know what that will mean. You had better make up your minds quickly, for there is no time to lose."

For some moments they remained silent. Then Maguire said sullenly: "Bedad, sir, since there's nothing else for it, I consent."

"And so do I," said Rooney. "Where's the paper?"

Carne handed them a formidable-looking document, and they read it in turn with ostentatious care. As soon as they had professed themselves willing to append their signatures to it, the sham detective took it to a writing-table at the other end of the room, and then ordered them to be unmanacled, so that they could come up in turn and sign. Had they been less agitated it is just possible they would have noticed that two sheets of blotting paper covered the context, and that only a small space on the paper, which was of a blueish grey tint, was left uncovered.

Then placing them in charge of the police officials, Carne left the room and went upstairs to examine their baggage. Evidently he discovered there what he wanted to know, for when he returned to the room his face was radiant.

Half an hour later they had left the house in separate cabs. Rooney was accompanied by Belton and one of his subordinates, now in plain clothes, while Carne and another took charge of

Maguire. At Euston they found special carriages awaiting them, and the same procedure was adopted in Ireland. The journey to Queenstown proved entirely uneventful; not for one moment did the two men suspect the trick that was being played upon them; nevertheless, it was with ill-concealed feelings of satisfaction that Carne and Belton bade them farewell upon the deck of the outward-bound steamer.

"Good-bye," said Maguire, as their captors prepared to pass over the side again. "An' good luck to ye. I'll wish ye that, for ye've treated us well, though it's a scurvy trick ye've played us in turning us out of England like this. First, however, one question. What about O'Grady?"

"The same course will be pursued with him, as soon as he is able to move," answered the other. "I can't say more."

"A word in your ear first," said Rooney. He leant towards Carne. "The girl's a good one" he said. "An' ye may do what ye can for her, for she knows nought of our business."

"I'll remember that if ever the chance arises," said Carne. "Now, good-bye."

"Good-bye."

On the Wednesday morning following, an elderly gentleman, dressed in rather an antiquated fashion, but boasting an appearance of great respectability, drove up in a brougham to the branch of the United Kingdom Bank in Oxford Street, and presented a cheque for no less a sum than forty-five thousand pounds, signed with the names of Septimus O'Grady, James Maguire, and Patrick Rooney, and bearing the date of the preceding Friday.

The cheque was in perfect order, and, in spite of the largeness of the amount, it was cashed without hesitation.

That afternoon Klimo received a visit from Mrs. Jeffreys. She came to express her gratitude for his help, and to ask the extent of her debt.

"You owe me nothing but your gratitude. I will not take a halfpenny. I am quite well enough rewarded now," said Klimo with a smile.

When she had gone he took out his pocket-book and consulted it.

"Forty-five thousand pounds," he said with a chuckle. "Yes, that is good. I did not take her money, but I *have* been rewarded in another way."

Then he went into Porchester House and dressed for the Garden Party at Marlborough House, to which he had been invited.

CHAPTER 4

THE WEDDING GUEST

One bright summer morning Simon Carne sat in his study, and reflected on the slackness of things in general. Since he had rendered such a signal service to the State, as narrated in the previous chapter, he had done comparatively nothing to raise himself in his own estimation. He was thinking in this strain when his butler entered, and announced "Kelmare Sahib." The interruption was a welcome one, and Carne rose to greet his guest with every sign of pleasure on his face.

"Good-morning, Kelmare," he said, as he took the other's outstretched hand; "I'm delighted to see you. How are you this morning?"

"As well as a man can hope to be under the circumstances," replied the new arrival, a somewhat *blasé* youth, dressed in the height of fashion. "You are going to the Greenthorpe wedding, of course. I hear you have been invited."

"You are quite right; I have," said Carne, and presently produced a card from the basket, and tossed it across the table.

The other took it up with a groan.

"Yes," he said, "that's it, by Jove! And a nice-looking document it is. Carne, did you ever hate anybody so badly that it seemed as if it would be scarcely possible to discover anything you would not do to hurt them?"

"No," answered Carne, "I cannot say that I have. Fate has always found me some way or another in which I might get even with my enemies. But you seem very vindictive in this matter. What's the reason of it?"

"Vindictive?" said Kelmare, "of course I am; think how they have treated me. A year ago, this week, Sophie Greenthorpe and I were engaged. Old Greenthorpe had not then turned his business into a limited liability company, and my people were jolly angry with me for making such a foolish match; but I did not care. I was in love, and Sophie Greenthorpe is as pretty a girl as can be found in the length and breadth of London. But there, you've seen her, so you know for yourself. Well, three months later, old Greenthorpe sold his business for upwards of three million sterling. On the strength of it he went into the House, gave thirty thousand to the funds of his party, and would have received a baronetcy for his generosity, had his party not been shunted out of power.

"Inside another month all the swells had taken them up; dukes and earls were as common at the old lady's receptions as they had been scarce before, and I began to understand that, instead of being everybody to them as I had once been, the old fellow was beginning to think his daughter might have done much better than become engaged to the third son of an impecunious earl.

"Then Kilbenham came upon the scene. He's a fine-looking fellow, and a marquis, but, as you know as well as I do, a real bad hat. He hasn't a red cent in the world to bless himself with, and he wanted money—well—just about as badly as a man *could* want it. What's the result? Within six weeks I am thrown over, and she has accepted Kilbenham's offer of marriage. Society says—'What a good match!' and, as if to endorse it, you received an invitation to the ceremony."

"Forgive me, but *you* are growing cynical now," said Carne, as he lit a fresh cigar.

"Haven't I good cause to be?" asked Kelmare. "Wait till you've been treated as I have, and then we'll see how you'll feel. When I think how every man you meet speaks of Kilbenham, and of the stories that are afloat concerning him, and hear the way old Greenthorpe and his pretensions are laughed at in the clubs, and sneered at in the papers, and am told that they are receiving presents of enormous value from all sorts and conditions of people, from Royalty to the poor devils of workmen he still under-pays, just because Kilbenham is a marquis and she is the daughter of a millionaire, why, I can tell you it is enough to make any one cynical."

"In the main, I agree with you," said Carne. "But, as life is made up of just such contradictions, it seems to me absurd to butt your head against a stone wall, and then grumble because it hurts and you don't make any impression on it. Do you think the presents are as wonderful as they say? I want to know, because I've not given mine yet. In these days one gives as others give. If they have not received anything very good, then a pair of electroplated entrée dishes will meet the case. If the reverse—well—diamonds, perhaps, or an old Master that the Americans are wild to buy, and can't."

"Who is cynical now, I should like to know?" said Kelmare. "I was told this morning that up to the present, with the superb diamonds given by the bride's father, they have totalled a value of something like twenty thousand pounds."

"You surprise me," answered Carne.

"I am surprised myself," said Kelmare, as he rose to go. "Now, I must be off. I came in to see if you felt inclined for a week's cruise in the Channel. Burgrave has lent me his yacht, and somehow I think a change of air will do me good."

"I am very sorry," said Carne, "but it would be quite impossible for me to get away just now. I have several important functions on hand that will keep me in town."

"I suppose this wedding is one of them?"

"To tell the honest truth, I had scarcely thought of it," replied Carne. "Must you be off? Well, then, good-bye, and a pleasant holiday to you."

When Kelmare had disappeared, Carne went back to his study, and seated himself at his writing-table. "Kelmare is a little over-sensitive," he said, "and his pique is spoiling his judgment. He does not seem to realize that he has come very well out of a jolly bad business. I am not certain which I pity most—Miss Greenthorpe, who is a heartless little hussy, or the Marquis of Kilbenham, who is a thorough-paced scoundrel. The wedding, however, promises to be a fashionable one, and——"

He stopped midway, rose, and stood leaning against the mantelpiece, staring into the empty fireplace. Presently he flipped the ash off his cigar, and turned round. "It never struck me in that light before," he said, as he pressed the button of the electric bell in the wall beside him. When it was answered, he ordered his carriage, and a quarter of an hour later was rolling down Regent Street.

Reaching a well-known jeweller's shop, he pulled the check string, and, the door having been opened, descended, and went inside. It was not the first time he had had dealings with the firm, and as soon as he was recognised the proprietor hastened forward himself to wait upon him.

"I want a nice wedding present for a young lady," he said, when the other had asked what he could have the pleasure of showing him. "Diamonds, I think, for preference."

A tray containing hairpins, brooches, rings, and aigrettes set with stones was put before him, but Carne was not satisfied. He wanted something better, he said—something a little more imposing. When he left the shop a quarter of an hour later he had chosen a diamond bracelet, for which he had paid the sum of one thousand pounds. In consequence, the jeweller bowed him to his carriage with almost Oriental obsequiousness.

As Carne rolled down the street, he took the bracelet from its case and glanced at it. He had long since made up his mind as to his line of action, and having done so, was now prepared to start business without delay. On leaving the shop, he had ordered his coachman to drive home; but on second thoughts he changed his mind, and, once more pulling the check string, substituted Berkeley Square for Park Lane.

"I must be thoroughly convinced in my own mind," he said, "before I do anything, and the only way to do that will be to see old Greenthorpe himself without delay. I think I have a good and sufficient excuse in my pocket. At any rate, I'll try it."

On reaching the residence in question, he instructed his footman to inquire whether Mr. Greenthorpe was at home, and if so, if he would see him. An answer in the affirmative was soon forthcoming, and a moment later Carne and Greenthorpe were greeting each other in the library.

"Delighted to see you, my dear sir," the latter said as he shook his guest warmly by the hand, at the same time hoping that old Sir Mowbray Mowbray next door, who was a gentleman of the old school, and looked down on the plutocracy, could see and recognise the magnificent equipage standing before his house. "This is most kind of you, and indeed I take it as most friendly too."

Carne's face was as smiling and fascinating as it was wont to be, but an acute observer might have read in the curves of his lips a little of the contempt he felt for the man before him. Matthew Greenthorpe's face and figure betrayed his origin as plainly as any words could have done. If this had not been sufficient, his dress and the profusion of jewellery—principally diamonds—that decked his person would have told the tale. In appearance he was short, stout, very red about the face, and made up what he lacked in breeding by an effusive familiarity that sometimes bordered on the offensive.

"I am afraid," said Carne, when his host had finished speaking, "that I ought to be ashamed of myself for intruding on you at such an early hour. I wanted, however, to thank you personally for the kind invitation you have sent me to be present at your daughter's wedding."

"I trust you will be able to come," replied Mr. Greenthorpe a little anxiously, for he was eager that the world should know that he and the now famous Simon Carne were on familiar terms.

"That is exactly what has brought me to see you," said Carne. "I regret to say I hardly know yet whether I shall be able to give myself that pleasure or not. An important complication has arisen in connection with some property in which I am interested, and it is just possible that I shall be called to the Continent within the next few days. My object in calling upon you this morning was to ask you to permit me to withhold my answer until I am at liberty to speak more definitely as to my arrangements."

"By all means, by all means," answered his host, placing himself with legs wide apart upon the hearthrug, and rattling the money in his trouser pockets. "Take just as long as you like

so long as you don't say you can't come. Me and the missus—
hem! I mean Mrs. Greenthorpe and I—are looking forward to
the pleasure of your society, and I can tell you we shan't think
our company complete if we don't have you with us."

"I am extremely flattered," said Carne sweetly, "and you
may be sure it will not be my fault if I am *not* among your
guests."

"Hear, hear, to that, sir," replied the old gentleman. "We
shall be a merry party, and, I trust, a distinguished one. We
did hope to have had Royalty present among us, but, unfortunately, there were special reasons, that I am hardly privileged
to mention, which prevented it. However, the Duke of Rugby
and his duchess, the father and mother of my future son-in-
law, you know, are coming; the Earl of Boxmoor and his
countess have accepted; Lord Southam and his lady, half a
dozen baronets or so, and as many Members of Parliament
and their wives as you can count on one hand. There'll be a
ball the night before, given by the Mayor at the Assembly
Rooms, a dinner to the tenants at the conclusion of the ceremony, and a ball in my own house after the young couple have
gone away. You may take it from me, my dear sir, that nothing
on a similar scale has ever been seen at Market Stopford
before."

"I can quite believe it," said Carne. "It will mark an epoch
in the history of the county."

"It will do more than that, sir. The festivities alone will cost
me a cool five thousand pounds. At first *I* was all for having it
in town, but I was persuaded out of it. After all, a country
house is better suited to such jinks. And we mean to do it
well."

He took Carne familiarly by the button of his coat, and,
sinking his voice to an impressive whisper, asked him to haz-
ard a guess how much he thought the whole affair, presents
and all, would cost.

Carne shook his head. "I have not the very remotest notion,"
he said. "But if you wish me to guess, I will put it at fifty thousand pounds."

"Not enough by half, sir—not enough by half. Why, I'll let

you into a little secret that even my wife knows nothing about."

As he spoke, he crossed the room to a large safe in the wall. This he unlocked, and having done so took from it an oblong box, wrapped in tissue paper. This he placed on the table in the centre of the room, and then, having looked out into the hall to make sure that no one was about, shut and locked the door. Then, turning to Carne, he said:

"I don't know what you may think, sir, but there are some people I know as try to insinuate that if you have money you can't have taste. Now, I've got the money"—here he threw back his shoulders, and tapped himself proudly on the chest—"and I'm going to convince you, sir, that I've got as pretty an idea of taste as any man could wish to have. This box will prove it."

So saying, he unwrapped the tissue paper, and displayed to Carne's astonished gaze a large gilded casket, richly chased, standing upon four massive feet.

"There, sir, you see," he said, "an artistic bit of workmanship, and I'll ask you to guess what it's for."

Carne, however, shook his head. "I'm afraid I'm but a poor hand at guessing, but, if I must venture an opinion, I should say a jewel case."

Thereupon Mr. Greenthorpe lifted the lid.

"And you would be wrong, sir. I will tell you what it is for. That box has been constructed to contain exactly fifty thousand sovereigns, and on her wedding day it will be filled, and presented to the bride, as a token of her father's affection. Now, if that isn't in good taste, I shall have to ask you to tell me what is."

"I am astonished at your munificence," said Carne. "To be perfectly candid with you, I don't know that I have ever heard of such a present before."

"I thought you'd say so. I said to myself when I ordered that box, 'Mr. Carne is the best judge of what is artistic in England, and I'll take his opinion about it.'"

"I suppose your daughter has received some valuable presents?"

"Valuable, sir? Why, that's no name for it. I should put down what has come in up to the present at not a penny under twenty thousand pounds. Why, you may not believe it, sir, but Mrs. Greenthorpe has presented the young couple with a complete toilet-set of solid gold. I doubt if such another has been seen in this country before."

"I should say it would be worth a burglar's while to pay a visit to your house on the wedding day," said Carne with a smile.

"He wouldn't get much for his pains," said the old gentleman warmly. "I have already provided for that contingency. The billiard-room will be used as a treasure-chamber for the time being, as there is a big safe like that over yonder in the wall. This week bars are being placed on all the windows, and on the night preceding, and also on the wedding day, one of my gardeners will keep watch in the room itself, while one of the village policemen will mount guard at the door in the passage. Between them they ought to be sufficient to keep out any burglars who may wish to try their hands upon the presents. What do you think?"

At that moment the handle of the door turned, and an instant later the bride-elect entered the room. On seeing Simon Carne she paused upon the threshold with a gesture of embarrassment, and made as if she would retreat. Carne, however, was too quick for her. He advanced and held out his hand.

"How do you do, Miss Greenthorpe?" he said, looking her steadily in the face. "Your father has just been telling me of the many beautiful presents you have received. I am sure I congratulate you most heartily. With your permission I will add my mite to the list. Such as it is, I would beg your acceptance of it."

So saying, he took from his pocket the case containing the bracelet he had that morning purchased. Unfastening it, he withdrew the circlet and clasped it upon her wrist. So great was her surprise and delight that for some moments she was at a loss how to express her thanks. When she recovered her presence of mind and her speech, she attempted to do so, but Carne stopped her.

"You must not thank me too much," he said, "or I shall begin to think I have done a meritorious action. I trust Lord Kilbenham is well?"

"He was very well when I last saw him," answered the girl after a momentary pause, which Carne noticed, "but he is so busy just now that we see very little of each other. Good-bye."

All the way home Simon Carne sat wrapped in a brown study. On reaching his residence he went straight to his study, and to his writing-desk, where he engaged himself for some minutes jotting down certain memoranda on a sheet of note-paper. When he had finished he rang the bell and ordered that Belton, his valet, should be sent to him.

"Belton," he said, when the person he wanted had arrived in answer to the summons, "on Thursday next I shall go down to Market Stopford to attend the wedding of the Marquis of Kilbenham with Miss Greenthorpe. You will, of course, accompany me. In the meantime" (here he handed him the sheet of paper upon which he had been writing) "I want you to attend to these few details. Some of the articles, I'm afraid, you will find rather difficult to obtain, but at any cost I must have them to take down to the country with me."

Belton took the paper and left the room with it, and for the time being Carne dismissed the matter from his mind.

The sun was in the act of setting on the day immediately preceding the wedding when Simon Carne and his faithful valet reached the wayside station of Market Stopford. As the train came to a standstill, a footman wearing the Greenthorpe livery opened the door of the reserved carriage and informed his master's guest that a brougham was waiting outside the station to convey him to his destination. Belton was to follow with the luggage in the servants' omnibus.

On arrival at Greenthorpe Park, Simon Carne was received by his host and hostess in the hall, the rearmost portion of which was furnished as a smoking-room. Judging from the number of guests passing, re-passing, and lolling about in the easy chairs, most of the company invited had already arrived. When he had greeted those with whom he was familiar, and had taken a cup of tea from the hands of the bride-elect, who was dispensing it at a small table near the great oak fireplace, he set himself to be agreeable to those about him for the space of a quarter of an hour, after which he was escorted to his bedroom, a pretty room situated in the main portion of the building at the head of the grand staircase. He found Belton awaiting him there. His luggage had been unpacked, and a glance at his watch told him that in a few minutes' time it would be necessary for him to prepare for dinner.

"Well, Belton," he said, as he threw himself into a chair beside the window that looked out over the rose garden, "here we are, and the next question is, how are we going to succeed?"

"I have never known you fail yet, sir," replied the deferential valet, "and I don't suppose you'll do so on this occasion."

"You flatter me, Belton, but I will not be so falsely modest as to say that your praise is altogether undeserved. This, however, is a case of more than usual delicacy and danger, and it will be necessary for us to play our cards with considerable care. When I have examined this house I shall elaborate my plans more fully. We have none too much time, for the attempt must be made to-morrow night. You have brought down with you the things I mentioned on that list, I suppose?"

"They are in these chests, sir," said Belton. "They make a precious heavy load, and once or twice I was fearful lest they might arouse suspicion."

"You need have no fear, my good Belton," said Carne. "I have a very plausible excuse to account for their presence here. Every one by this time knows that I am a great student, and also that I never travel without at least two cases of books. It is looked upon as a harmless fad. Here is my key. Open the box standing nearest to you."

Belton did as he was commanded, when it was seen that it was filled to its utmost holding capacity with books.

"No one would think," said Carne, with a smile at the astonishment depicted on the other's face, "that there are only two layers of volumes there, would they? If you lift out the tray upon which they rest, you will discover that the balance of the box is now occupied by the things you placed in it.

Unknown to you, I had the trays fitted after you had packed the others. There is nothing like being prepared for all emergencies. Now, pay attention to what I am about to say to you. I have learned that the wedding presents, including the fifty thousand sovereigns presented by Mr. Greenthorpe to his daughter in that absurd casket, of which I spoke to you, will be on view to-morrow afternoon in the billiard-room; to-night, and to-morrow before the ball commences, they will be placed in the safe. One of Mr. Greenthorpe's most trusted servants will keep watch over them in the room, while a constable will be on duty in the lobby outside. Bars have been placed on all the windows, and, as I understand, the village police will patrol the building at intervals during the night. The problem of how we are to get hold of them would seem rather a hard nut to crack, would it not?"

"I must confess I don't see how you are going to do it at all, sir," said Belton.

"Well, we'll see. I have a plan in my head now, but before I can adopt it I must make a few inquiries. I believe there is a staircase leading from the end of this corridor down to the lobby outside the billiard and smoking-rooms. If this is so, we shall have to make use of it. It must be your business to discover at what time the custodians of the treasure have their last meal. When you have found that out let me know. Now you had better get me ready for dinner as soon as possible."

When Carne retired to rest that evening, his inimitable valet was in a position to report that the sentries were already installed, and that their supper had been taken to them, by Mr. Greenthorpe's orders, at ten o'clock precisely, by one of the under-footmen, who had been instructed to look after them.

"Very good," said Carne; "I think I see my way now. I'll sleep on my scheme and let you know what decision I have come to in the morning. If we pull this little business off successfully, there will be ten thousand pounds for you to pay into your credit, my friend."

Belton bowed and thanked his master without a sign of emotion upon his face. After which Simon Carne went to bed.

When he was called next morning, he discovered a perfect summer day. Brilliant sunshine streamed in at the windows, and the songs of birds came from the trees outside.

"An excellent augury," he said to himself as he jumped out of bed and donned the heavy dressing-gown his valet held open for him. "Miss Greenthorpe, my compliments to you. My lord marquis is not the only man upon whom you are conferring happiness to-day."

His good humour did not leave him, for when he descended to the breakfast-room an hour later his face was radiant with smiles, and every one admitted that it would be impossible to meet a more charming companion.

During the morning he was occupied in the library, writing letters.

At one he lunched with his fellow-guests, none of the family being present, and at half-past went off to dress for the wedding ceremony. This important business completed, a move was made for the church; and in something less than a quarter of an hour the nuptial knot was tied, and Miss Sophie Greenthorpe, only daughter of Matthew Greenthorpe, erstwhile grocer and provision merchant, of Little Bexter Street, Tottenham Court Road, left the building, on her husband's arm, Marchioness of Kilbenham and future Duchess of Rugby.

Simon Carne and his fellow-guests followed in her wake down the aisle, and, having entered their carriages, returned to the Park.

The ball that evening was an acknowledged success, but, though he was an excellent dancer, and had his choice of the prettiest women in the room, Carne was evidently ill at ease. The number of times he stealthily examined his watch said this as plainly as any words. As a matter of fact, the last guest had scarcely arrived before he left the ball-room, and passed down the lobby towards the back staircase, stopping *en route* to glance at the billiard-room door.

As he expected, it was closed, and a stalwart provincial policeman stood on guard before it.

He made a jocular reference about the treasure the constable was guarding, and, with a laugh at himself for forgetting the way to his bedroom, retraced his steps to the stairs, up which he passed to his own apartment. Belton was awaiting him there.

"It is ten minutes to ten, Belton," he said abruptly. "It must be now or never. Go down to the kitchen, and hang about there until the tray upon which the suppers of the guard are placed is prepared. When the footman starts with it for the billiard-room, accompany him, and, as he opens the green baize door leading from the servants' quarters into the house, manage, by hook or crook, to hold him in conversation. Say something, and interrupt yourself by a severe fit of coughing. That will give me my cue. If anything should happen to me as I come downstairs, be sure that the man puts his tray down on the slab at the foot of the stairs and renders me assistance. I will manage the rest. Now be off."

Belton bowed respectfully, and left the room. As he did so, Carne crossed to the dressing-table, and unlocked a small case standing upon it. From this he took a tiny silver-stoppered scent bottle, containing, perhaps, half an ounce of white powder. This he slipped into his waistcoat pocket, and then made for the door.

On the top of the back staircase he paused for a few moments to listen. He heard the spring of the green baize door in the passage below creak as it was pushed open. Next moment he distinguished Belton's voice. "It's as true as that I'm standing here," he was saying. "As I went up the stairs with the governor's hot water there she was coming along the passage. I stood back to let her pass, and as I did she——" (Here the narrative was interrupted by a violent fit of coughing.) On hearing this Carne descended the stairs, and, when he had got half-way down, saw the footman and his valet coming along the passage below. At the same instant he must have caught his foot in the stair carpet, for he tripped and fell headlong to the bottom.

"Heaven's alive!" cried Belton. "I do believe that's my governor, and he's killed." At the same time he ran forward to the injured man's assistance.

Carne lay at the foot of the stairs just as he had fallen, his head thrown back, his eyes shut, and his body curled up and

motionless. Belton turned to the footman, who still stood holding the tray where he had stopped on seeing the accident, and
said: "Put down those things and go and find Mr. Greenthorpe
as quickly as you can. Tell him Mr. Carne has fallen downstairs, and I'm afraid is seriously injured."

The footman immediately disappeared. His back was
scarcely turned, however, before Carne was on his feet.

"Excellent, my dear Belton," he whispered; and, as he spoke,
he slipped his fingers into his waistcoat pocket. "Hand me up
that tray, but be quiet, or the policeman round the corner will
hear you."

Belton did as he was ordered, and Carne thereupon sprinkled
upon the suppers provided for the two men some of the white
powder from the bottle he had taken from his dressing-case.
This done, he resumed his place at the foot of the stairs, while
Belton, kneeling over him and supporting his head, waited for
assistance. Very few minutes elapsed before Mr. Greenthorpe,
with his scared face, appeared upon the scene. At his direction
Belton and the footman carried the unconscious gentleman to
his bedroom, and placed him upon his bed. Restoratives were
administered, and in something under ten minutes the injured
man once more opened his eyes.

"What is the matter?" he asked feebly. "What has happened?"

"You have met with a slight accident, my dear sir," said the
old gentleman, "but you are better now. You fell downstairs."

As if he scarcely comprehended what was said, Carne feebly
repeated the last sentence after his host, and then closed his
eyes again. When he opened them once more, it was to beg
Mr. Greenthorpe to leave him and return to his guests downstairs. After a small amount of pressing, the latter consented
to do so, and retired, taking the footman with him. The first
use Carne made of their departure was to turn to Belton.

"The powder will take effect in five hours," he said. "See
that you have all the things prepared."

"They are quite ready," replied Belton. "I arranged them
this evening."

"Very good," said Carne. "Now, I am going to sleep in real
earnest."

So saying, he closed his eyes, and resigned himself to slumber as composedly as if nothing out of the common had occurred. The clock on the stables had struck three when he woke again. Belton was still sleeping peacefully, and it was not until he had been repeatedly shaken that he became conscious that it was time to get up.

"Wake up," said Carne; "it is three o'clock, and time for us to be about our business. Unlock that box, and get out the things."

Belton did as he was ordered, placing the packets as he took them from the cases in small Gladstone bags. Having done this, he went to one of his master's trunks, and took from it two suits of clothes, a pair of wigs, two excellently contrived false beards, and a couple of soft felt hats. These he placed upon the bed. Ten minutes later he had assisted his master to change into one of the suits, and when this was done waited for further instructions.

"Before you dress, take a tumbler from that table, and go downstairs. If you should meet any one, say that you are going to the butler's pantry in search of filtered water, as you have used all the drinking water in this room. The ball should be over by this time, and the guests in bed half an hour ago. Ascertain if this is the case, and as you return glance at the policeman on duty outside the billiard-room door. Let me know his condition."

"Very good, sir," said Belton; and, taking a tumbler from the table in question, he left the room. In less than five minutes he had returned to report that, with the exception of the corridor outside the billiard-room, the house was in darkness.

"And how is the guardian of the door?" Carne inquired.

"Fast asleep," said Belton, "and snoring like a pig, sir."

"That is right," said Carne. "The man inside should be the same, or that powder has failed me for the first time in my experience. We'll give them half an hour longer, however, and then get to work. You had better dress yourself."

While Belton was making himself up to resemble his master, Carne sat in an easy chair by his dressing-table, reading Ruskin's "Stones of Venice." It was one of the most important of his many peculiarities that he could withdraw his thoughts from any subject, however much it might hitherto have engrossed him, and fasten them upon another, without once allowing them to wander back to their original channel. As the stable clock chimed the half-hour, he put the book aside, and sprang to his feet.

"If you're ready, Belton," he said, "switch off the electric light and open that door."

When this had been done he bade his valet wait in the bed-room while he crept down the stairs on tip-toe. On turning into the billiard-room lobby, he discovered the rural police-man propped up in the corner fast asleep. His heavy breathing echoed down the corridors, and one moment's inspection showed Carne that from him he had nothing to fear. Unlock-ing the door with a key which he took from his pocket, he entered the room, to find the gardener, like the policeman, fast asleep in an armchair by the window. He crossed to him, and, after a careful examination of his breathing, lifted one of his eyelids.

"Excellent," he said. "Nothing could be better. Now, when Belton comes, we shall be ready for business."

So saying, he left the room again, and went softly up the stairs to find his valet. The latter was awaiting him, and, before a witness, had there been one, could have counted twenty, they were standing in the billiard-room together. It was a large apartment, luxuriously furnished, with a bow window at one end and an alcove, surrounded with seats, at the other. In this alcove, cleverly hidden by the wainscotting, as Mr. Greenthorpe had once been at some pains to point out to Simon Carne, there existed a large iron safe of the latest burglar-proof pattern and design.

The secret was an ingenious one, and would have baffled any ordinary craftsman. Carne, however, as has already been explained, was far from being a common-place member of his profession. Turning to Belton, he said, "Give me the tools." These being forthcoming, in something less than ten minutes he had picked the lock and was master of the safe's contents.

When these, including the fifty thousand sovereigns, had

been safely carried upstairs and stowed away in the portman-teaux and chests, and the safe had been filled with the spuri-ous jewellery he had brought with him for that purpose, he signed to Belton to bring him a long pair of steps which stood in a corner of the room, and which had been used for securing the sky-light above the billiard table. These he placed in such a position as would enable him to reach the window.

With a diamond-pointed instrument, and a hand as true as the eye that guided it, he quickly extracted a square of col-oured glass, filed through the catch, and was soon standing on the leads outside. A few moments later, the ladder, which had already rendered him such signal service, had enabled him to descend into the garden on the other side.

There he arranged a succession of footsteps in the soft mould, and having done so, returned to the roof, carefully wiped the end of the ladder, so that it should not betray him, and climbed down into the room below, pulling it after him.

"I think we have finished now," he said to Belton, as he took a last look at the recumbent guardians of the room. "These gentlemen sleep soundly, so we will not disturb them further. Come, let us retire to bed."

In less than half an hour he was in bed and fast asleep. Next morning he was still confined to his room by his accident, though he expressed himself as suffering but slight pain. Every one was quick to sympathise with him, and numerous mes-sages were conveyed to him expressive of sorrow that he should have met with his accident at such a time of general rejoicing. At ten o'clock the first batch of guests took their departure. It was arranged that the Duke and Duchess of Rugby, the Earl and Countess of Raxter, and Simon Carne, who was to be carried downstairs, should travel up to town together by the special train leaving immediately after lunch.

When they bade their host good-bye, the latter was nearly overcome.

"I'm sure it has been a real downright pleasure to me to entertain you, Mr. Carne," he said, as he stood by the carriage door and shook his guest warmly by the hand. "There is only one thing bad about it, and that is your accident."

"You must not speak of that," said Carne, with a little wave of his hand. "The pleasure I have derived from my visit to you amply compensates me for such a minor inconvenience."

So saying he shook hands and drove away to catch his train.

Next morning it was announced in all the Society papers that, owing to an unfortunate accident he had sustained while visiting Mr. Matthew Greenthorpe, at Greenthorpe Park, on the occasion of his daughter's marriage, Mr. Simon Carne would be unable to fulfil any of the engagements he might have entered into.

Any intelligent reader of the aforesaid papers might have been excused had he pictured the gentleman in question confined to his bed, tended by skilled nurses, and watched over by the most fashionable West End physicians obtainable for love or money. They would doubtless, therefore, have been surprised could they have seen him at a late hour on the following evening hard at work in the laboratory he had constructed at the top of his house, as hale and hearty a man as any to be found in the great Metropolis.

"Now those Apostle spoons," he was saying, as he turned from the crucible at which he was engaged to Belton, who was busy at a side table. "The diamonds are safely disposed of, their settings are melted down, and, when these spoons have been added to the list, he will be a wise man who can find in my possession any trace of the famous Kilbenham-Greenthorpe wedding presents."

He was sitting before the fire in his study next morning, with his left foot lying bound up upon a neighbouring chair, when Ram Gafur announced "Kelmare Sahib."

"So sorry to hear that you are under the weather, Carne," said the new-comer as he shook hands. "I only heard of your accident from Raxter last night, or I should have been round before. Beastly hard luck, but you shouldn't have gone to the wedding, you know!"

"And, pray, why not?"

"You see for yourself you haven't profited by your visit, have you?"

"That all depends upon what you consider profit," replied

Carne. "I was an actor in an interesting Society spectacle. I was permitted an opportunity of observing my fellow-creatures in many new lights. Personally, I think I did very well. Besides that, to be laid up just now is not altogether a thing to be despised, as you seem to imagine."

"What do you mean?"

"It isn't everybody who can boast such a valid excuse for declining invitations as I now possess," said Carne. "When I tell you that I had a dinner, a lecture at the Imperial Institute, two 'at homes,' and three dances on my list for to-night, you will understand what I mean. Now I am able to decline every one of them without risk of giving offence or fear of hurting the susceptibilities of any one. If you don't call that luck, I do. And now tell me what has brought you here, for I suppose you have some reason, other than friendship, for this early call. When you came in I observed that you were bursting with importance. You are not going to tell me that you have abandoned your yachting trip and are going to be married?"

"You need have no fear on that score. All the same, I have the greatest and most glorious news for you. It isn't every day a man finds Providence taking up his case and entering into judgment against his enemies for him. That is my position. Haven't you heard the news?"

"What news?" asked Carne innocently.

"The greatest of all possible news," answered Kelmare, "and one which concerns you, my dear fellow. You may not believe it, but it was discovered last evening that the Kilbenham-Greenthorpe wedding presents have all been stolen, including the fifty thousand sovereigns presented to the bride in the now famous jewelled casket. What do you think of that?"

"Surely you must be joking," said Carne incredulously. "I cannot believe it."

"Nevertheless it's a fact," replied Kelmare.

"But when did it happen? and how did they discover it?" asked Carne.

"When it took place nobody can tell, but they discovered it when they came to put the presents together after the guests had departed. On the morning after the wedding old

Greenthorpe had visited the safe himself, and glanced casually at its contents, just to see that they were all right, you know; but it was not until the afternoon, when they began to do them up, that they discovered that every single article of value the place contained had been abstracted, and dummies substituted. Their investigation proved that the sky-light had been tampered with, and one could see unmistakable footmarks on the flower beds outside.

"Good gracious!" said Carne. "This is news indeed. What a haul the thieves must have had, to be sure! I can scarcely believe it even now. But I thought they had a gardener in the room, a policeman at the door, and a patrol outside, and that old Greenthorpe went to sleep with the keys of the room and safe under his pillow?"

"Quite right," said Kelmare, "so he did; that's the mysterious part of it. The two chaps swear positively that they were wide awake all night, and that nothing was tampered with while they were there. Who the thieves were, and how they became so familiar with the place, are riddles that it would puzzle the Sphinx, or your friend Klimo next door, to unravel."

"What an unfortunate thing," said Carne. "It's to be hoped the police will catch them before they have time to dispose of their booty."

"You are thinking of your bracelet, I suppose?"

"It may seem egotistical, but I must confess I was; and now I suppose you'll stay to lunch?"

"I'm afraid that's impossible. There are at least five families who have not heard the news, and I feel that it is my bounden duty to enlighten them."

"You're quite right, it is not often a man has such glorious vengeance to chronicle. It behoves you to make the most of it."

The other looked at Carne as if to discover whether or not he was laughing at him. Carne's face, however, was quite expressionless.

"Good-bye; I suppose you won't be at the Wilbringham's to-night?"

"I'm afraid not. You evidently forget that, as I said just now, I have a very good and sufficient excuse."

When the front door had closed behind his guest, Carne lit a third cigar.

"I'm overstepping my allowance," he said reflectively, as he watched the smoke circle upward, "but it isn't every day a man gives a thousand pounds for a wedding present and gets upwards of seventy thousand back. I think I may congratulate myself on having brought off a very successful little speculation."

CHAPTER 5

A CASE OF PHILANTHROPY

If one consults a dictionary one finds that the word dipso-maniac means a man who spends his life continually desiring alcoholic liquor; a name that properly classifies it has not yet been invented for the individual who exhibits a perpetual crav-ing for notoriety, and yet one is, perhaps, as much a nuisance to society as the other. After his run of success there came a time when Simon Carne, like Alexander the Great, could have sat down and wept, for the reason that he had no more worlds to conquer. For the moment it seemed as if he had exhausted, to put it plainly, every species of artistic villainy.

He had won the Derby, under peculiar circumstances, as narrated elsewhere; he had rendered a signal, though an unos-tentatious, service to the State; he had stolen, under enormous difficulty, the most famous family jewels in Europe; and he had relieved the most fashionable bride and bridegroom of the season of the valuable presents that their friends and relations had lavished on them.

Having accomplished so much, it would seem as if he had done all that mortal man could do to create a record for him-self, but, like the dipsomaniac above mentioned, he was by no means satisfied, he craved for more. It delighted him beyond all measure to hear the comments of his friends upon each daring crime as it became known to the world. What he wanted now was something before which all the rest would sink into insignificance. Day after day he had puzzled his brains, but without success. All he wanted was a hint. When he got it he could be trusted to follow it up for himself. At present, however, even that was wanting.

On a morning following a banquet at the Mansion House, at which he had been a welcome, as well as a conspicuous guest, he was sitting alone in his study smoking a meditative cigar. Though the world would scarcely have thought it, a fashionable life did not suit him, and he was beginning to wonder whether he was not, after all, a little tired of England. He was hungering for the warmth and colour of the East, and, perhaps, if the truth must be told, for something of the rest he had known in the Maharajah of Kadir's lake palace, where he had been domiciled when he had first made the acquaintance of the man who had been his sponsor in English society, the Earl of Amberley.

It was a strange coincidence that, while he was thinking of that nobleman, and of the events which had followed the introduction just referred to, his quick ears should have caught the sound of a bell that was destined eventually to lead him up to one of the most sensational adventures of all his sensational career. A moment later his butler entered to inform him that Lady Caroline Weltershall and the Earl of Amberley had called, and would like to see him. Tossing his cigar into the grate, he passed through the door Ram Gafur held open for him, and, having crossed the hall, entered the drawing-room.

As he went he wondered what it was that had brought them to see him at such an early hour. Both were among his more intimate acquaintances, and both occupied distinguished positions in the social life of the world's great metropolis. While her friends and relations spent their time in search of amusement, and a seemingly eternal round of gaieties, which involved a waste of both health and money, Lady Caroline, who was the ugly duckling of an otherwise singularly handsome family, put her life to a different use.

Philanthropy was her hobby, and scarcely a day passed in which she did not speak at some meeting, preside over some committee, or endeavour in some way, as she somewhat grandiloquently put it: "To better the lives and ameliorate the conditions of our less fortunate fellow creatures." In appearance she was a short, fair woman, of about forty-five years of age, with a not unhandsome face, the effect of which, however, was completely spoilt by two large and protruding teeth.

"My dear Lady Caroline, this is indeed kind of you," said Carne, as he shook hands with her, "and also of you, Lord Amberley. To what happy circumstance may I attribute the pleasure of this visit?"

"I fear it is dreadfully early for us to come to see you," replied her ladyship, "but Lord Amberley assured me that as our business is so pressing you would forgive us."

"Pray do not apologise," returned Carne. "It gives me the greatest possible pleasure to see you. As for the hour I am ashamed to confess that, while the morning is no longer young, I have only just finished breakfast. But won't you sit down?"

They seated themselves once more, and when they had done so, Lady Caroline unfolded her tale.

"As you are perhaps aware, my friends say that I never come to see them unless it is to attempt to extort money from them for some charitable purpose," she said. "No, you need not prepare to button up your pockets, Mr. Carne. I am not going to ask you for anything to-day. What I *do* want, however, is to endeavour to persuade you to help us in a movement we are inaugurating to raise money with which to relieve the great distress in the Canary Islands, brought about by the late disastrous earthquake. My cousin, the Marquis of Laverstock, has kindly promised to act as president, and, although we started it but yesterday, ten thousand pounds have already been subscribed. As you are aware, however, if we are to attract public attention and support, the funds raised must be representative of all classes. Our intention, therefore, is to hold a drawing-room meeting at my house to-morrow afternoon, when a number of the most prominent people of the day will be invited to give us their views upon the subject.

"I feel sure, if you will only consent to throw in your lot with us, and to assist in carrying out what we have in view, we shall be able to raise a sum of at least one hundred thousand pounds for the benefit of the sufferers. Our kind friend here, Lord Amberley, has promised to act as secretary, and his efforts will be invaluable to us. Royalty has signified its gracious approval, and it is expected will head the list with a handsome donation. Every class will be appealed to. Ministers of religion, of all known denominations, will be invited to co-operate, and if you will only consent to allow your name to appear upon the *personnel* of the committee, and will allow us to advertise your name as a speaker at to-morrow's meeting, I feel sure there is nothing we shall not be able to achieve."

"I shall be delighted to help you in any way I can," Carne replied. "If my name is likely to be of any assistance to you, I beg you will make use of it. In the meantime, if you will permit me, I will forward you a cheque for one thousand pounds, being my contribution to the fund you have so charitably started."

Her ladyship beamed with delight, and even Lord Amberley smiled gracious approval.

"You are generous, indeed," said Lady Caroline. "I only wish others would imitate your example."

She did not say that, wealthy though she herself was, she had only contributed ten pounds to the fund. It is well known that while she inaugurated large works of charity, she seldom contributed very largely to them. As a wit once remarked: "Philanthropy was her virtue, and meanness was her vice."

"Egad," said Amberley, "if you're going to open your purse strings like that, Carne, I shall feel called upon to do the same."

"Then let me have the pleasure of booking both amounts at once," cried her ladyship, at the same time whipping out her note-book and pencil with flattering alacrity.

"I shall be delighted," said Carne, with a smile of eagerness.

"I also," replied Amberley, and in a trice both amounts were written down. Having gained her point, her ladyship rose to say good-bye. Lord Amberley immediately imitated her example.

"You will not forget, will you, Mr. Carne?" she said. "I am to have the pleasure of seeing you at my house to-morrow afternoon at three o'clock. We shall look forward to hearing your speech, and I need not remind you that every word you utter will be listened to with the closest attention."

"At three to-morrow afternoon," said Carne, "I shall be at your house. You need have no fear that I shall forget. And now, since you think you must be going, good-bye, and many thanks to you for asking me."

He escorted them to the carriage which was waiting outside, and when he had watched it drive away, returned to his study to write the cheque he had promised her. Having done so, he did not rise from his chair, but continued to sit at his writing-table, biting the feather of his quill pen and staring at the blotting pad before him. A great and glorious notion had suddenly come into his head, and the majesty of it was for the moment holding him spellbound.

"If only it could be worked," he said to himself, "what a glorious *coup* it would be. The question for my consideration is, can it be done? To invite the people of England to subscribe its pounds, shillings, and pence, for my benefit, would be a glorious notion, and just the sort of thing I should enjoy. Besides which I have to remember that I am a thousand pounds to the bad already, and that must come back from somewhere. For the present, however, I'll put the matter aside. After the meeting to-morrow I shall have something tangible to go upon, and then, if I still feel in the same mind, it will be strange if I can't find some way of doing what I want. In the meantime I shall have to think out my speech; upon that will depend a good deal of my success. It is a strange world in which it is ordained that so much should depend upon so little!"

At five minutes to three o'clock on the following afternoon Simon Carne might have been observed—that, I believe, is the correct expression—strolling across from Apsley House to Gloucester Place. Reaching Lord Weltershall's residence, he discovered a long row of carriages lining the pavement, and setting down their occupants at his lordship's door. Carne followed the stream into the house, and was carried by it up the stairs towards the large drawing-room where the meeting was to be held. Already about a hundred persons were present, and it was evident that, if they continued to arrive at the same rate, it would not be long before the room would be filled to over-flowing. Seeing Lady Caroline bidding her friends welcome near the door, Carne hastened to shake hands with her.

"It is so very good of you to come," she said, as she took his hand. "Remember, we are looking to you for a rousing speech this afternoon. We want one that will inflame all England,

and touch the heart-strings of every man and woman in the land."

"To touch their purse-strings would, perhaps, be more to the point," said Carne, with one of his quiet smiles.

"Let us hope we shall touch them, too," she replied. "Now would you mind going to the dais at the other end of the room? You will find Lord Laverstock there, talking to my husband, I think."

Carne bowed, and went forward as he had been directed.

So soon as it was known that the celebrities had arrived, the meeting was declared open and the speechmaking commenced. Clever as some of them were it could not be doubted that Carne's address was the event of the afternoon. He was a born speaker, and what was more, despite the short notice he had received, had made himself thoroughly conversant with his subject. His handsome face was on fire with excitement, and his sonorous voice rang through the large room like a trumpet call. When he sat down it was amidst a burst of applause. Lord Laverstock leant forward and shook hands with him.

"Your speech will be read all over England to-morrow morning," he said. "It should make a difference of thousands of pounds to the fund. I congratulate you most heartily upon it."

Simon Carne felt that if it was really going to make that difference he might, in the light of future events, heartily congratulate himself. He, however, accepted the praise showered upon him with becoming modesty, and, during the next speaker's exhibition of halting elocution, amused himself watching the faces before him, and speculating as to what they would say when the surprise he was going to spring upon them became known. Half an hour later, when the committee had been elected and the meeting had broken up, he bade his friends good-bye and set off on his return home. That evening he was dining at home, intending to call at his club afterwards, and to drop in at a reception and two dances between ten and midnight. After dinner, however, he changed his mind, and having instructed Ram Gafur to deny him to all callers, and countermanding his order for his carriage, went to his study, where he locked himself in and sat down to smoke and think.

He had set himself a puzzle which would have taxed the brain of that arch schemer Machiavelli himself. He was not, however, going to be beaten by it. There *must* be some way, he told himself, in which the fraud could be worked, and if there was he was going to find it. Numberless were the plans he formed, only to discover a few moments later that some little difficulty rendered each impracticable.

Suddenly, throwing down the pencil with which he had been writing, he sprang to his feet and began eagerly to pace the room. It was evident, from the expression upon his face, that he had touched upon a train of thought that was at last likely to prove productive. Reaching the fireplace for about the thirtieth time, he paused and gazed into the fireless grate. After standing there for a few moments he turned, and, with his hands in his pockets, said solemnly to himself: "Yes! I think it *can* be done!"

Whatever the train of thought may have been that led him to make this declaration, it was plain that it afforded him no small amount of satisfaction. He did not, however, commit himself at once to a decision, but continued to think over the scheme he had hit upon until he had completely mastered it. It was nearly midnight before he was thoroughly satisfied. Then he followed his invariable practice on such occasions, and rang for the inimitable Belton. When he had admitted him to the room, he bade him close and lock the door behind him.

By the time this had been done he had lit a fresh cigar, and had once more taken up his position on the hearthrug.

"I sent for you to say that I have just made up my mind to try a little scheme, compared with which all I have done so far will sink into insignificance."

"What is it, sir?" asked Belton.

"I will tell you, but you must not look so terrified. Put in a few words, it is neither more nor less than to attempt to divert the enormous sum of money which the prodigal English public is taking out of its pocket in order to assist the people of the Canary Islands, who have lost so severely by the recent terrible earthquake, into my own."

Belton's face expressed his astonishment.

"But, my dear sir," he said, "that's a fund of which the Marquis of Laverstock is president, and of whose committee you are one of the principal members."

"Exactly," answered Carne. "It is to those two happy circumstances I shall later on attribute the success I now mean to attain. Lord Laverstock is merely a pompous old nobleman, whose hobby is philanthropy. This lesson will do him good. It will be strange if, before I am a week older, I cannot twist him round my finger. Now for my instructions. In the first place, you must find me a moderate-sized house, fit for an elderly lady, and situated in a fairly fashionable quarter, say South Kensington. Furnish it on the hire system from one of the big firms, and engage three servants who can be relied upon to do their work, and what is more important, who can hold their tongues.

"Next find me an old lady to impersonate the mistress of the house. She must be very frail and delicate-looking, and you will arrange with some livery stable people in the neighbourhood to supply her with a carriage, in which she will go for an airing every afternoon in order that the neighbourhood may become familiar with her personality. Both she and the servants must be made to thoroughly understand that their only chance of obtaining anything from me depends upon their carrying out my instructions to the letter. Also, while they are in the house, they must keep themselves to themselves. My identity, of course, must not transpire.

"As soon as I give the signal, the old lady must keep to the house, and the neighbourhood must be allowed to understand that she is seriously ill. The day following she will be worse, and the next she will be dead. You will then make arrangements for the funeral, order a coffin, and arrange for the conveyance of the body to Southampton, *en route* for the Channel Islands, where she is to be buried. At Southampton a yacht, which I will arrange for myself, will be in readiness to carry us out to sea. Do you think you understand?"

"Perfectly, sir," Belton replied, "but I wish I could persuade you to give up the attempt. You will excuse my saying so, sir, I hope, but it does seem to me a pity, when you have done so much, to risk losing it all over such a dangerous bit of business as this. It surely can't succeed, sir?"

"Belton," said Carne very seriously, "you strike me as being in a strange humour to-night, and I cannot say that I like it, Were it not that I have the most implicit confidence in you, I should begin to think you were turning honest. In that case our connection would be likely to be a very short one."

"I hope, sir," Belton answered in alarm, "that you still believe I am as devoted as ever to your interests."

"I do believe it," Carne replied. "Let the manner in which you carry out the various instructions I have just given you, confirm me in that belief. This is Wednesday. I shall expect you to come to me on Saturday with a report that the house has been taken and furnished, and that the servants are installed and the delicate old lady in residence."

"You may rely upon my doing my best, sir."

"I feel sure of that," said Carne, "and now that all is arranged I think that I will go to bed."

A week later a committee of the Canary Islands Relief Fund was able to announce to the world, through the columns of the Daily Press, that the generous public of England had subscribed no less a sum than one hundred thousand pounds for the relief of the sufferers by the late earthquake. The same day Carne attended a committee meeting in Gloucester Place. A proposition advanced by Lady Weltershall and seconded by Simon Carne was carried unanimously. It was to the effect that in a week's time such members of the Relief Committee as could get away should start for the scene of the calamity in the chairman's yacht, which had been placed at their disposal, taking with them, for distribution among the impoverished inhabitants of the Islands, the sum already subscribed, namely, one hundred thousand pounds in English gold. They would then be able, with the assistance of the English Consul, to personally superintend the distribution of their money, and also be in a position to report to the subscribers, when they returned to England, the manner in which the money had been utilised.

"In that case," said Carne, who had not only seconded the

motion, but had put the notion into Lady Weltershall's head, "it might be as well if our chairman would interview the authorities of the bank, and arrange that the amount in question shall be packed, ready for delivery to the messengers he may select to call for it before the date in question."

"I will make it my business to call at the bank to-morrow morning," replied the chairman, "and perhaps you, Mr. Carne, would have no objection to accompany me."

"If it will facilitate the business of this committee I shall be only too pleased to do so," said Carne, and so it was settled.

On a Tuesday afternoon, six days later, and two days before the date upon which it had been arranged that the committee should sail, the Marquis of Laverstock received a letter. Lady Caroline Weltershall, the Earl of Amberley, and Simon Carne were with him when he opened it. He read it through, and then read it again, after which he turned to his guests.

"This is really a very extraordinary communication," he said, "and as it affects the matter we have most at heart, perhaps I had better read it to you:

> 154, Great Chesterton Street,
> Tuesday Evening.

To the Most Noble the Marquis of Laverstock, K.G., Berkeley Square.

My Lord—As one who has been permitted to enjoy a long and peaceful life in a country where such visitations are happily unknown, I take the liberty of writing to your Lordship to say how very much I should like to subscribe to the fund so nobly started by you and your friends to assist the poor people who have lost so much by the earthquake in the Canary Islands. Being a lonely old woman, blessed by Providence with some small share of worldly wealth, I feel it my duty to make some small sacrifice to help others who have not been so blessed.

Unfortunately, I do not enjoy very good health, but if your Lordship could spare a moment to call upon me, I would like to thank you in the name of Womanhood for all you have done, and, in proof of my gratitude, would willingly give you my cheque for the sum of ten thousand pounds to add to the amount already subscribed. I am permitted by my doctors to see visitors between the hours of eleven and twelve in the morning, and five and six in the afternoon. I should then be both honoured and pleased to see your Lordship.

Trusting you will concede me this small favour, I have the honour to be,

Yours very sincerely,
JANET O'HALLORAN.

There was a momentary pause after his lordship had finished reading the letter.

"What will you do?" inquired Lady Caroline.

"It is a noble offering," put in Simon Carne.

"I think there cannot be two opinions as to what is my duty," replied the chairman. "I shall accede to her request, though why she wants to see me is more than I can tell."

"As she hints in the letter, she wishes to congratulate you personally on what you have done," continued the Earl of Amberley; "and as it will be the handsomest donation we have yet received, it will, perhaps, be as well to humour her."

"In that case I will do as I say, and make it my business to call there this afternoon between five and six. And now it is my duty to report to you that Mr. Simon Carne and I waited upon the authorities at the Bank this morning, and have arranged that the sum of one hundred thousand pounds in gold shall be ready for our messengers when they call for it, either to-morrow morning or to-morrow afternoon at latest."

"It is a large sum to take with us," said Lady Caroline. "I trust it will not prove a temptation to thieves!"

"You need have no fear on that score," replied his lordship. "As I have explained to the manager, my own trusted servants will effect the removal of the money, accompanied by two private detectives, who will remain on board my yacht until we weigh anchor. We have left nothing to chance. To make the matter doubly sure, I have also arranged that the money shall not be handed over except to a person who shall present my cheque, and at the same time show this signet ring which I now wear upon my finger."

The other members of the committee expressed themselves as perfectly satisfied with this arrangement, and when certain other business had been transacted the meeting broke up.

As soon as he left Berkeley Square Carne returned with all haste to Porchester House. Reaching his study he ordered that Belton should be at once sent to him.

"Now, Belton," he said, when the latter stood before him, "there is not a moment to lose. Lord Laverstook will be at Great Chesterton Street in about two hours. Send a messenger to Waterloo to inquire if they can let us have a special train at seven o'clock to take a funeral party to Southampton. Use the name of Merryburn, and you may say that the amount of the charge, whatever it may be, will be paid before the train starts. As soon as you obtain a reply, bring it to 154, Great Chesterton Street. In the meantime I shall disguise myself and go on to await you there. On the way I shall wire to the captain of the yacht at Southampton to be prepared for us. Do you understand what you have to do?"

"Perfectly, sir," Belton replied. "But I must confess that I am very nervous."

"There is no need to be. Mark my words, everything will go like clockwork. Now I am going to change my things and prepare for the excursion."

He would have been a sharp man who would have recognised in the dignified-looking clergyman who drove up in a hansom to 154, Great Chesterton Street, half an hour later, Simon Carne, who had attended the committee meeting of the Canary Island Relief Fund that afternoon. As he alighted he looked up, and saw that all the blinds were drawn down, and that there were evident signs that Death had laid his finger on the house. Having dismissed his cab he rang the bell, and when the door was opened entered the house. The butler who admitted him had been prepared for his coming. He bowed respectfully, and conducted him to the drawing-room. There he found an intensely respectable old lady, attired in black silk, seated beside the window.

"Go upstairs," he said peremptorily, "and remain in the room above this until you are told to come down. Be careful not to let yourself be seen. As soon as it gets dark to-night you can leave the house, but not till then. Before you go the money promised you will be paid. Now be off upstairs, and make sure that none of the neighbours catch sight of you."

Ten minutes later a man, who might have been a retired military officer, and who was dressed in deepest black, drove up, and was admitted to the house. Though no one would have recognised him, Carne addressed him at once as "Belton."

"What have you arranged about the train?" he asked, as soon as they were in the drawing-room together.

"I have settled that it shall be ready to start for Southampton punctually at seven o'clock," the other answered.

"And what about the hearse?"

"It will be here at a quarter to seven, without fail."

"Very good; we will have the corpse ready meanwhile. Now, before you do anything else, have the two lower blinds in the front drawn up. If he thinks there is trouble in the house he may take fright, and we must not scare our bird away after all the bother we have had to lure him here."

For the next hour they were busily engaged perfecting their arrangements. These were scarcely completed before a gorgeous landau drove up to the house, and Belton reported that the footman had alighted and was ascending the steps.

"Let his lordship be shown into the drawing-room," said Simon Carne, "and as soon as he is there do you, Belton, wait at the door. I'll call you when I want you."

Carne went into the drawing-room and set the door ajar. As he did so he heard the footman inquire whether Mrs. O'Halloran was at home, and whether she would see his master. The butler answered in the affirmative, and a few moments later the Marquis ascended the steps.

"Will you be pleased to step this way, my lord," said the servant. "My mistress is expecting you, and will see you at once."

When he entered the drawing-room he discovered the same portly, dignified clergyman whom the neighbours had seen enter the house an hour or so before, standing before the fireplace.

"Good-afternoon, my lord," said this individual, as the door closed behind the butler. "If you will be good enough to take a seat, Mrs. O'Halloran will be down in a few moments."

His lordship did as he was requested, and while doing so commented on the weather, and allowed his eyes to wander round the room. He took in the grand piano, the easy chairs on either side of the book-case, and the flower-stand in the window. He could see that there was plain evidence of wealth in these things. What his next thought would have been can only be conjectured, for he was suddenly roused from his reverie by hearing the man say in a gruff voice: "It's all up, my lord. If you move or attempt to cry out, you're a dead man!"

Swinging round he discovered a revolver barrel pointed at his head. He uttered an involuntary cry of alarm, and made as if he would rise.

"Sit down, sir," said the clergyman authoritatively. "Are you mad that you disobey me? You do not know with whom you are trifling."

"What do you mean?" cried the astonished peer, his eyes almost starting from his head. "I demand to be told what this behaviour means. Are you aware who I am?"

"Perfectly," the other replied. "As to your other question, you will know nothing more than I choose tell you. What's more, I should advise you to hold your tongue, unless you desire to be gagged. That would be unpleasant for all parties."

Then, turning to the door, he cried: "Come in, Dick!"

A moment later the military individual, who had been to Waterloo to arrange about the train, entered the room to find the Most Noble the Marquis of Laverstock seated in an easy chair, almost beside himself with terror, with the venerable clergyman standing over him revolver in hand.

"Dick, my lad," said the latter quietly, "his lordship has been wise enough to hear reason. No, sir, thank you, your hands behind your back, as arranged, if you please. If you don't obey me I shall blow your brains out, and it would be a thousand pities to spoil this nice Turkey carpet. That's right. Now Dick, my lad, I want his lordship's pocket-book from his coat and those sheets of note-paper and envelopes we brought with us. I carry a stylographic pen myself, so there is no need of ink."

These articles having been obtained, they were placed on a table beside him, and Carne took possession of the pocket-book. He leisurely opened it, and from it took the cheque for one hundred thousand pounds, signed by the chairman and committee of the Canary Island Relief Fund, which had been drawn that afternoon.

"Now take the pen," he said, "and begin to write. Endeavour to remember that I am in a hurry, and have no time to waste. Let the first letter be to the bank authorities. Request them, in your capacity of Chairman of the Relief Fund, to hand to the bearers the amount of the cheque in gold."

"I will do no such thing," cried the old fellow sturdily. "Nothing shall induce me to assist you in perpetrating such a fraud."

"I am sorry to hear that," said Carne sweetly, "for I am afraid in that case we shall be compelled to make you submit to a rather unpleasant alternative. Come, sir, I will give you three minutes in which to write that letter. If at the end of that time you have not done so, I shall proceed to drastic measures."

So saying, he thrust the poker into the fire in a highly suggestive manner. Needless to say, within the time specified the letter had been written, placed in its envelope, and directed.

"Now I shall have to trouble you to fill in this telegraph form to your wife, to tell her that you have been called out of town, and do not expect to be able to return until to-morrow."

The other wrote as directed, and when he had done so Carne placed this paper also in his pocket.

"Now I want that signet ring upon your finger, if you please."

The old gentleman handed it over to his persecutor with a heavy sigh. He had realized that it was useless to refuse.

"Now that wine-glass on the sideboard, Dick," said the clergyman, "also that carafe of water. When you have given them to me, go and see that the other things I spoke to you about are ready."

Having placed the articles in question upon the table Belton left the room. Carne immediately filled the glass, into which he poured about a tablespoonful of some dark liquid from a bottle which he took from his pocket, and which he had brought with him for that purpose.

"I'll have to trouble you to drink this, my lord," he said, as he stirred the contents of the glass with an ivory paper knife taken from the table. "You need have no fear. It is perfectly harmless, and will not hurt you."

"I will not touch it," replied the other. "Nothing you can do or say will induce me to drink a drop of it."

Carne examined his watch ostentatiously.

"Time flies, I regret to say," he answered impressively, "and I cannot stay to argue the question with you. I will give you three minutes to do as I have ordered you. If you have not drunk it by that time we shall be compelled to repeat the little persuasion we tried with such success a few moments since."

"You wish to kill me," cried the other. "I will not drink it. I will not be murdered. You are a fiend to attempt such a thing."

"I regret to say you are wasting time," replied his companion. "I assure you if you drink it you will not be hurt. It is merely an opiate intended to put you to sleep until we have time to get away in safety. Come, that delightful poker is getting hot again, and if you do not do what I tell you, trouble will ensue. Think well before you refuse."

There was another pause, during which the unfortunate nobleman gazed first at the poker, which had been thrust between the bars of the grate, and then at the relentless being who stood before him, revolver in hand. Never had a member of the House of Lords been placed in a more awkward and unenviable position.

"One minute," said Carne quietly.

There was another pause, during which the Marquis groaned in a heartrending manner. Carne remembered with a smile that the family title had been bestowed upon one of the Marquis' ancestors for bravery on the field of battle.

"Two minutes!"

As he spoke he stooped and gave the poker a little twist.

"Three minutes!"

The words were scarcely out of his mouth before Lord Laverstock threw up his hands.

"You are a heartless being to make me, but I will drink," he cried, and with an ashened face he immediately swallowed the contents of the glass.

"Thank you," said Carne politely.

The effect produced by the drug was almost instantaneous. A man could scarcely have counted a hundred before the old gentleman, who had evidently resigned himself to his fate, laid himself back in his chair and was fast asleep.

"He has succumbed even quicker than I expected," said Carne to himself as he bent over the prostrate figure and listened to his even breathing. "It is, perhaps, just as well that this drug is not known in England. At any rate, on this occasion it has answered my purpose most admirably."

At five minutes before seven o'clock a hearse containing the mortal remains of Mrs. O'Halloran, of Great Chesterton Street, South Kensington, entered the yard of Waterloo Station, accompanied by a hansom cab. A special train was in waiting to convey the party, which consisted of the deceased's brother, a retired Indian officer, and her cousin, the vicar of a Somersetshire parish, to Southampton, where a steam yacht would transport them to Guernsey, in which place the remains were to be interred beside those of her late husband.

"I think we may congratulate ourselves, Belton, on having carried it out most successfully," said Carne when the coffin had been carried on board the yacht and placed in the saloon. "As soon as we are under weigh we'll have this lid off and get the poor old gentleman out. He has had a good spell of it in there, but he may congratulate himself that the ventilating arrangements of his temporary home were so perfectly attended to. Otherwise I should have trembled for the result."

A few hours later, having helped his guest to recover consciousness, and having seen him safely locked up in a cabin on board, the yacht put in at a little seaport town some thirty or forty miles from Southampton Water, and landed two men in time to catch the midnight express to London. The following afternoon they rejoined the yacht a hundred miles or so further down the coast. When they were once more out at sea Carne called the skipper to his cabin.

"How has your prisoner conducted himself during our absence?" he asked. "Has he given any trouble?"

"Not a bit," replied the man. "The poor old buffer's been too sick to make a row. He sent away his breakfast and his lunch untouched. The only thing he seems to care about is champagne, and that he drinks by the bottle full. I never saw a better man at his bottle in all my life."

"A little sickness will do him no harm; he'll have a better appetite when he gets on dry land again," said Carne. "His time is pretty well up now, and as soon as it is dark to-night we'll put him ashore. Let me know when you sight the place."

"Very good, sir," replied the skipper, and immediately he returned to the deck again.

It was well after ten o'clock that evening when Simon Carne, still attired as a respectable Church of England clergyman, unlocked the door and entered his prisoner's cabin.

"You will be glad to hear, my lord," he said, "that your term of imprisonment has at last come to an end. You had better get up and dress, for a boat will be alongside in twenty minutes to take you ashore."

The unfortunate gentleman needed no second bidding. Ill as he had hitherto been, he seemed to derive new life from the other's words. At any rate, he sprang out of his bunk, and set to work to dress with feverish energy. All the time Carne sat and watched him with an amused smile upon his face. So soon as he was ready, and the captain had knocked at the door, he was conducted to the deck and ordered to descend into a shore boat, which had come off in answer to a signal, and was now lying alongside in readiness.

Carne and Belton leant over the bulwarks to watch him depart.

"Good-bye, my lord," cried the former, as the boat moved away. "It has been a sincere pleasure to me to entertain you, and I only hope that, in return, you have enjoyed your little excursion. You might give my respectful compliments to the members of the Canary Island Relief Fund, and tell them that there is at least one person on board this yacht who appreciates their kindly efforts."

Then his lordship stood up, and shook his fist at the yacht until it had faded away, and could no longer be seen owing to the darkness. Presently Carne turned to Belton.

"So much for the Most Noble the Marquis of Laverstock," he said, "and the Canary Island Relief Fund. Now, let us be off to town. To-morrow I must be Simon Carne once more."

Next morning Simon Carne rose from his couch, in his luxurious bedroom, a little later than usual. He knew he should be tired, and had instructed Belton not to come in until he rang his bell. When the latter appeared he bade him bring in the morning papers. He found what he wanted in the first he opened, on the middle page, headed with three lines of large type:

GIGANTIC SWINDLE.
THE MARQUIS OF LAVERSTOCK ABDUCTED.
THE CANARY ISLAND RELIEF FUND STOLEN.

"This looks quite interesting," said Carne, as he folded the paper in order to be able the better to read the account. "As I know something of the case I shall be interested to see what they have to say about it. Let me see."

The newspaper version ran as follows:

Of all the series of extraordinary crimes which it has been our unfortunate duty to chronicle during this year of great rejoicing, it is doubtful whether a more impudent robbery has been perpetrated than that which we have to place before our readers this morning. As every one is well aware, a large fund has been collected from all classes for the relief of the sufferers by the recent Canary Island earthquake. On the day before the robbery took place this fund amounted to no less a sum than one hundred thousand pounds, and to-morrow it was the intention of the committee, under the presidency of the Most Noble the Marquis of Laverstock, to proceed to the seat of the disaster, taking with them the entire amount of the sum raised in English gold. Unfortunately for the success of this scheme, his lordship was the recipient, two days ago, of a letter from a person purporting to reside in Great Chesterton Street, South Kensington. She signed herself Janet O'Halloran, and offered to add a sum of ten thousand pounds to the amount already collected, provided the Marquis would call and collect her cheque personally. The excuse given for this extraordinary stipulation was that she wished to convey to him her thanks for the trouble he had taken.

Accordingly, feeling that he had no right to allow such a chance to slip, his lordship visited the house. He was received in the drawing-room by a man dressed in the garb of a clergyman, who, assisted by a military-looking individual, presently clapped a revolver to his head and demanded, under the threat of all sorts of penalties, that he should give up to him the cheque drawn upon the Bank, and which it was the Marquis's intention to have cashed the following morning. Not satisfied with this assurance, he was also made to write an order to the banking authorities authorising them to pay over the money to the bearer, who was a trusted agent, while at the same time he was to supply them with his signet ring, which, as had already been arranged, would prove that the messengers were genuine and what they pretended to be. Next he was ordered to drink a powerful opiate, and after that his lordship remembers nothing more until he woke to find himself on board a small yacht in mid-channel. Despite the agony he was suffering, he was detained on board this piratical craft until late last night, when he was set ashore at a small village within a few miles of Plymouth. Such is his lordship's story. The sequel to the picture is as follows.

Soon after the Bank was opened yesterday, a respectable-looking individual, accompanied by three others, who were introduced to the manager as private detectives, put in an appearance and presented the Relief Fund's cheque at the

counter. In reply to inquiries the letter written by the Marquis
was produced, and the signet ring shown. Never for a moment
doubting that these were the messengers the Bank had all along
been told to expect, the money was handed over and placed in a
handsome private omnibus which was waiting outside. It was
not until late last night, when a telegram was received from the
Marquis of Laverstock from Plymouth, that the nature of the
gigantic fraud which had been perpetrated was discovered.
The police authorities were immediately communicated with
and the matter placed in their hands. Unfortunately, however,
so many hours had been allowed to elapse that it was extremely
difficult to obtain any clue that might ultimately lead to the
identification of the parties concerned in the fraud. So far the
case bids fair to rank with those other mysterious robberies
which, during the last few months, have shocked and puzzled all
England.

"I regard that as a remarkably able exposition of the case,"
said Carne to himself with a smile as he laid the paper down,
"but what an account the man would be able to write if only
he could know what is in my safe upstairs!"

That afternoon he attended a committee meeting of the
fund at Weltershall House. The unfortunate nobleman whose
unpleasant experience has founded the subject of this story
was present. Carne was among the first to offer him an expression of sympathy.

"I don't know that I ever heard of a more outrageous case,"
he said. "I only hope that the scoundrels may be soon brought
to justice."

"In the meantime what about the poor people we intended
to help?" asked Lady Weltershall.

"They shall not lose," replied Lord Laverstock. "I shall
refund the entire amount myself."

"No, no, my lord; that would be manifestly unfair," said
Simon Carne. "We are all trustees of the fund, and what happened is as much our fault as yours. If nine other people will
do the same I am prepared to contribute a sum of ten thousand
pounds towards the fund."

"I will follow your example," said the Marquis.

"I also," continued Lord Amberley.

By nightfall seven other gentlemen had done the same, and, as Simon Carne said as he totalled the amounts: "By this means the Canary Islanders will not be losers after all."

CHAPTER 6

AN IMPERIAL FINALE

Of all the functions that ornament the calendar of the English social and sporting year, surely the Cowes week may claim to rank as one of the greatest, or at least the most enjoyable. So thought Simon Carne as he sat on the deck of Lord Tremorden's yacht, anchored off the mouth of the Medina River, smoking his cigarette and whispering soft nothings into the little shell-like ear of Lady Mabel Madderley, the lady of all others who had won the right to be considered the beauty of the past season. It was a perfect afternoon, and, as if to fill his flagon of enjoyment to the very brim, he had won the Queen's Cup with his yacht, *The Unknown Quantity*, only half an hour before. Small wonder, therefore, that he was contented with his lot in life, and his good fortune of that afternoon in particular.

The tiny harbour was crowded with shipping of all sorts, shapes, and sizes, including the guardship, his Imperial Majesty the Emperor of Westphalia's yacht the *Hohenszrallas*, the English Royal yachts, steam yachts, schooners, cutters, and all the various craft taking part in England's greatest water carnival. Steam launches darted hither and thither, smartly equipped gigs conveyed gaily-dressed parties from vessel to vessel, while, ashore, the little town itself was alive with bunting, and echoed to the strains of almost continuous music.

"Surely you ought to consider yourself a very happy man, Mr. Carne," said Lady Mabel Madderley, with a smile, in reply to a speech of the other's. "You won the Derby in June, and to-day you have appropriated the Queen's Cup."

"If such things constitute happiness, I suppose I must be in the seventh heaven of delight," answered Carne, as he took another cigarette from his case and lit it. "All the same, I am insatiable enough to desire still greater fortune. When one has set one's heart upon winning something, beside which the Derby and the Queen's Cup are items scarcely worth considering, one is rather apt to feel that fortune has still much to give."

"I am afraid I do not quite grasp your meaning," she said. But there was a look in her face that told him that, if she did not understand, she could at least make a very good guess. According to the world's reckoning, he was quite the best fish then swimming in the matrimonial pond, and some people, for the past few weeks, had even gone so far as to say that she had hooked him. It could not be denied that he had been paying her unmistakable attention of late.

What answer he would have vouchsafed to her speech it is impossible to say, for at that moment their host came along the deck towards them. He carried a note in his hand.

"I have just received a message to say that his Imperial Majesty is going to honour us with a visit," he said, when he reached them. "If I mistake not, that is his launch coming towards us now."

Lady Mabel and Simon Carne rose and accompanied him to the starboard bulwarks. A smart white launch, with the Westphalian flag flying at her stern, had left the Royal yacht and was steaming quickly towards them. A few minutes later it had reached the companion ladder, and Lord Tremorden had descended to welcome his Royal guest. When they reached the deck together, his Majesty shook hands with Lady Tremorden, and afterwards with Lady Mabel and Simon Carne.

"I must congratulate you most heartily, Mr. Carne," he said, "on your victory to-day. You gave us an excellent race, and though I had the misfortune to be beaten by thirty seconds, still I have the satisfaction of knowing that the winner was a better boat in every way than my own."

"Your Majesty adds to the sweets of victory by your generous acceptance of defeat," Carne replied. "But I must confess that I owe my success in no way to my own ability. The boat was chosen for me by another, and I have not even the satisfaction of saying that I sailed her myself."

"Nevertheless she is your property, and you will go down to posterity famous in yachting annals as the winner of the Queen's Cup in this justly celebrated year."

With this compliment his Majesty turned to his hostess and entered into conversation with her, leaving his aide-de-camp free to discuss the events of the day with Lady Mabel. When he took his departure half an hour later, Carne also bade his friends good-bye, and, descending to his boat, was rowed away to his own beautiful steam yacht, which was anchored a few cables' length away from the Imperial craft. He was to dine on board the latter vessel that evening.

On gaining the deck he was met by Belton, his valet, who carried a telegram in his hand. As soon as he received it, Carne opened it and glanced at the contents, without, however, betraying very much interest.

An instant later the expression upon his face changed like magic. Still holding the message in his hand, he turned to Belton.

"Come below," he said quickly. "There is news enough here to give us something to think of for hours to come."

Reaching the saloon, which was decorated with all the daintiness of the upholsterer's art, he led the way to the cabin he had arranged as a study. Having entered it, he shut and locked the door.

"It's all up, Belton," he said. "The comedy has lasted long enough, and now it only remains for us to speak the tag, and after that to ring the curtain down as speedily as may be."

"I am afraid, sir, I do not quite take your meaning," said Belton. "Would you mind telling me what has happened?"

"I can do that in a very few words," the other answered. "This cablegram is from Trincomalee Liz, and was dispatched from Bombay yesterday. Read it for yourself."

He handed the paper to his servant, who read it carefully, aloud:

To CARNE, Porchester House, Park Lane, London.—Bradfield left fortnight since. Have ascertained that you are the object.

TRINCOMALEE.

"This is very serious, sir," said the other, when he had finished.

"As you say, it is very serious indeed," Carne replied. "Bradfield thinks he has caught me at last, I suppose; but he seems to forget that it is possible for me to be as clever as himself. Let me look at the message again. Left a fortnight ago, did he? Then I've still a little respite. By Jove, if that's the case, I'll see that I make the most of it."

"But surely, sir, you will leave at once," said Belton quickly. "If this man, who has been after us so long, is now more than half way to England, coming with the deliberate intention of running you to earth, surely, sir, you'll see the advisability of making your escape while you have time."

Carne smiled indulgently.

"Of course I shall escape, my good Belton," he said. "You have never known me neglect to take proper precautions yet; but before I go I must do one more piece of business. It must be something by the light of which all I have hitherto accomplished will look like nothing. Something really great, that will make England open its eyes as it has not done yet."

Belton stared at him, this time in undisguised amazement.

"Do you mean to tell me, sir," he said with the freedom of a privileged servant, "that you intend to run another risk, when the only man who knows sufficient of your career to bring you to book is certain to be in England in less than a fortnight? I cannot believe that you would be so foolish, sir. I beg of you to think what you are doing."

Carne, however, paid but small attention to his servant's intreaties.

"The difficulty," he said to himself, speaking his thoughts aloud, "is to understand quite what to do. I seem to have used up all my big chances. However, I'll think it over, and it will be strange if I don't hit upon something. In the meantime, Belton, you had better see that preparations are made for leaving England on Friday next. Tell the skipper to have everything ready. We shall have done our work by that time; then hey for the open sea and freedom from the trammels of a society life once more. You might drop a hint or two to certain people that I am going, but be more than careful what you say. Write to the agents about Porchester House, and attend to all the other necessary details. You may leave me now."

Belton bowed, and left the cabin without another word. He knew his master sufficiently well to feel certain that neither intreaties nor expostulations would make him abandon the course he had mapped out for himself. That being so, he bowed to the inevitable with a grace which had now become a habit to him.

When he was alone, Carne once more sat for upwards of an hour in earnest thought. He then ordered his gig, and, when it was ready, set out for the shore. Making his way to the telegraph office, he dispatched a message which at any other, and less busy, time, would have caused the operator some astonishment. It was addressed to a Mahommedan dealer in precious stones in Bombay, and contained only two words in addition to the signature. They were:

"Leaving—come."

He knew that they would reach the person for whom they were intended, and that she would understand their meaning and act accordingly.

The dinner that night on board the Imperial yacht *Hohenszrallas* was a gorgeous affair in every sense of the word. All the principal yacht owners were present, and, at the conclusion of the banquet, Carne's health, as winner of the great event of the regatta, was proposed by the Emperor himself, and drunk amid enthusiastic applause. It was a proud moment for the individual in question, but he bore his honours with that quiet dignity that had stood him in such good stead on so many similar occasions. In his speech he referred to his approaching departure from England, and this, the first inkling of such news, came upon his audience like a thunder-clap. When they had taken leave of his Majesty soon after midnight, and were standing on deck, waiting for their respective boats to draw up to the accommodation ladder, Lord Orpington made his way to where Simon Carne was standing.

"Is it really true that you intend leaving us so soon?" he asked.

"Quite true, unfortunately," Carne replied. "I had hoped to have remained longer, but circumstances over which I have no control make it imperative that I should return to India without delay. Business that exercises a vital influence upon my fortunes compels me. I am therefore obliged to leave without fail on Friday next. I have given orders to that effect this afternoon."

"I am extremely sorry to hear it, that's all I can say," said Lord Amberley, who had just come up. "I assure you we shall all miss you very much indeed."

"You have all been extremely kind," said Carne, "and I have to thank you for an exceedingly pleasant time. But, there, let us postpone consideration of the matter for as long as possible. I think this is my boat. Won't you let me take you as far as your own yacht?"

"Many thanks, but I don't think we need trouble you," said Lord Orpington. "I see my gig is just behind yours."

"In that case, good-night," said Carne. "I shall see you as arranged, to-morrow morning, I suppose?"

"At eleven," said Lord Amberley. "We'll call for you and go ashore together. Good-night."

By the time Carne had reached his yacht he had made up his mind. He had also hit upon a scheme, the daring of which almost frightened himself. If only he could bring it off, he told himself, it would be indeed a fitting climax to all he had accomplished since he had arrived in England. Retiring to his cabin, he allowed Belton to assist him in his preparations for the night almost without speaking. It was not until the other was about to leave the cabin that he broached the subject that was occupying his mind to the exclusion of all else.

"Belton," he said, "I have decided upon the greatest scheme that has come into my mind yet. If Simon Carne is going to say farewell to the English people on Friday next, and it succeeds, he will leave them a legacy to think about for some time after he has gone."

"You are surely not going to attempt anything further, sir," said Belton in alarm. "I *did* hope, sir, that you would have listened to my intreaties this afternoon."

"It was impossible for me to do so," said Carne. "I am afraid, Belton, you are a little lacking in ambition. I have noticed that on the last three occasions you have endeavoured to dissuade me from my endeavours to promote the healthy excitement of the English reading public. On this occasion fortunately I am able to withstand you. To-morrow morning you will commence preparations for the biggest piece of work to which I have yet put my hand."

"If you have set your mind upon doing it, sir, I am quite aware that it is hopeless for me to say anything," said Belton resignedly. "May I know, however, what it is going to be?"

Carne paused for a moment before he replied.

"I happen to know that the Emperor of Westphalia, whose friendship I have the honour to claim," he said, "has a magnificent collection of gold plate on board his yacht. It is my intention, if possible, to become the possessor of it."

"Surely that will be impossible, sir," said Belton. "Clever as you undoubtedly are in arranging these things, I do not see how you can do it. A ship at the best of times is such a public place, and they will be certain to guard it very closely."

"I must confess that at first glance I do not quite see how it is to be managed, but I have a scheme in my head which I think may possibly enable me to effect my purpose. At any rate, I shall be able to tell you more about it to-morrow. First, let us try a little experiment."

As he spoke he seated himself at his dressing-table, and bade Belton bring him a box which had hitherto been standing in a corner. When he opened it, it proved to be a pretty little cedarwood affair divided into a number of small compartments, each of which contained *crêpe* hair of a different colour. Selecting a small portion from one particular compartment, he unraveled it until he had obtained the length he wanted, and then with dexterous fingers constructed a moustache, which he attached with spirit gum to his upper lip. Two or three twirls gave it the necessary curl, then with a pair of ivory-backed brushes taken from the dressing-table he brushed his hair back in a peculiar manner, placed a hat of uncommon shape upon his head, took a heavy boat cloak from a cupboard near at hand, threw it round his shoulders, and, assuming an almost defiant expression, faced Belton, and desired him to tell him whom he resembled.

Familiar as he was with his master's marvellous power of disguise and his extraordinary faculty of imitation, the latter could not refrain from expressing his astonishment.

"His Imperial Majesty the Emperor of Westphalia," he said. "The likeness is perfect."

"Good," said Carne. "From that exhibition you will gather something of my plan. To-morrow evening, as you are aware, I am invited to meet his Majesty, who is to dine ashore accompanied by his aide-de-camp, Count Von Walzburg. Here is the latter's photograph. He possesses, as you know, a very decided personality, which is all in our favour. Study it carefully."

So saying, he took from a drawer a photograph, which he propped against the looking-glass on the dressing-table before him. It represented a tall, military-looking individual, with bristling eyebrows, a large nose, a heavy grey moustache, and hair of the same colour. Belton examined it carefully.

"I can only suppose, sir," he said, "that, as you are telling me this, you intend me to represent Count Von Walzburg."

"Exactly," said Carne. "That is my intention. It should not be at all difficult. The Count is just your height and build. You will only need the moustache, the eyebrows, the grey hair, and the large nose, to look the part exactly. To-morrow will be a dark night, and, if only I can control circumstances sufficiently to obtain the chance I want, detection, in the first part of our scheme at any rate, should be most unlikely, if not almost impossible."

"You'll excuse my saying so, I hope, sir," said Belton, "but it seems a very risky game to play when we have done so well up to the present."

"You must admit that the glory will be the greater, my friend, if we succeed."

"But surely, sir, as I said just now, they keep the plate you mention in a secure place, and have it properly guarded."

"I have made the fullest inquiries, you may be sure. It is kept in a safe in the chief steward's cabin, and, while it is on board,

a sentry is always on duty at the door. Yes, all things considered, I should say it is kept in a remarkably secure place."

"Then, sir, I'm still at a loss to see how you are going to
obtain possession of it."

Carne smiled indulgently. It pleased him to see how per-
plexed his servant was.

"In the simplest manner possible," he said, "provided always
that I can get on board the yacht without my identity being
questioned. The manner in which we are to leave the vessel
will be rather more dangerous, but not sufficiently so to cause
us any great uneasiness. You are a good swimmer, I know, so
that a hundred yards should not hurt you. You must also have
a number of stout canvas sacks, say six, prepared, and securely
attached to each the same number of strong lines; the latter
must be fifty fathoms long, and have at the end of each a stout
swivel hook. The rest is only a matter of detail. Now, what
have you arranged with regard to matters in town?"

"I have fulfilled your instructions, sir, to the letter," said
Belton. "I have communicated with the agents who act for the
owner of Porchester House. I have caused an advertisement to
be inserted in all the papers to-morrow morning to the effect
that the renowned detective, Klimo, will be unable to meet his
clients for at least a month, owing to the fact that he has
accepted an important engagement upon the Continent, which
will take him from home for that length of time. I have negoti-
ated the sale of the various horses you have in training, and I
have also arranged for the disposal of the animals and carriages you have now in use in London. Ram Gafur and the
other native servants at Porchester House will come down by
the midday train to-morrow, but before they do so, they will
fulfil your instructions and repair the hole in the wall between
the two houses. I cannot think of any more, sir."

"You have succeeded admirably, my dear Belton," said
Carne, "and I am very pleased. To-morrow you had better see
that a paragraph is inserted in all the daily papers announcing
the fact that it is my intention to leave England for India immediately, on important private business. I think that will do for
to-night."

Belton tidied the cabin, and, having done so, bade his master good-night. It was plain that he was exceedingly nervous about the success of the enterprise upon which Carne was embarking so confidently. The latter, on the other hand, retired to rest and slept as peacefully as if he had not a care or an anxiety upon his mind.

Next morning he was up by sunrise, and, by the time his friends Lords Orpington and Amberley were thinking about breakfast, had put the finishing touches to the scheme which was to bring his career in England to such a fitting termination.

According to the arrangement entered into on the previous day, his friends called for him at eleven o'clock, when they went ashore together. It was a lovely morning, and Carne was in the highest spirits. They visited the Castle together, made some purchases in the town, and then went off to lunch on board Lord Orpington's yacht. It was well-nigh three o'clock before Carne bade his host and hostess farewell, and descended the gangway in order to return to his own vessel. A brisk sea was running, and for this reason to step into the boat was an exceedingly difficult, if not a dangerous, matter. Either he miscalculated his distance, or he must have jumped at the wrong moment; at any rate, he missed his footing, and fell heavily on to the bottom. Scarcely a second, however, had elapsed before his coxswain had sprung to his assistance, and had lifted him up on to the seat in the stern. It was then discovered that he had been unfortunate enough to once more give a nasty twist to the ankle which had brought him to such grief when he had been staying at Greenthorpe Park on the occasion of the famous wedding.

"My dear fellow, I am so sorry," said Lord Orpington, who had witnessed the accident. "Won't you come on board again? If you can't walk up the ladder we can easily hoist you over the side."

"Many thanks," replied Carne, "but I think I can manage to get back to my own boat. It is better I should do so. My man has had experience of my little ailments, and knows exactly what is best to be done under such circumstances; but it is a terrible nuisance, all the same. I'm afraid it will be impossible for me now to be present at his Royal Highness's dinner this evening, and I have been looking forward to it so much."

"We shall all be exceedingly sorry," said Lord Amberley. "I shall come across in the afternoon to see how you are."

"You are very kind," said Carne, "and I shall be immensely glad to see you if you can spare the time."

With that he gave the signal to his men to push off. By the time he reached his own yacht his foot was so painful that it was necessary for him to be lifted on board—a circumstance which was duly noticed by the occupants of all the surrounding yachts, who had brought their glasses to bear upon him. Once below in his saloon, he was placed in a comfortable chair and left to Belton's careful attention.

"I trust you have not hurt yourself very much, sir," said that faithful individual, who, however, could not prevent a look of satisfaction coming into his face, which seemed to say that he was not ill-pleased that his master would, after all, be prevented from carrying out the hazardous scheme he had proposed to him the previous evening.

In reply, Carne sprang to his feet without showing a trace of lameness.

"My dear Belton, how peculiarly dense you are to-day," he said, with a smile, as he noticed the other's amazement. "Cannot you see that I have only been acting as you yourself wished I should do early this morning—namely, taking precautions? Surely you must see that, if I am laid up on board my yacht with a sprained ankle, society will say that is quite impossible for me to be doing any mischief elsewhere. Now, tell me, is everything prepared for to-night?"

"Everything, sir," Belton replied. "The dresses and wigs are ready. The canvas sacks, and the lines to which the spring hooks are attached, are in your cabin awaiting your inspection. As far as I can see, everything is prepared, and I hope will meet with your satisfaction."

"If you are as careful as usual, I feel sure it will," said Carne. "Now get some bandages and make this foot of mine up into as artistic a bundle as you possibly can. After that help me on deck and prop me up in a chair. As soon as my accident gets known there will be certain to be shoals of callers on board, and I must play my part as carefully as possible."

As Carne had predicted, this proved to be true. From half-past three until well after six o'clock a succession of boats drew up at his accommodation ladder, and the sufferer on deck was the recipient of as much attention as would have flattered the vainest of men. He had been careful to send a letter of apology to the illustrious individual who was to have been his host, expressing his sincere regrets that the accident which had so unfortunately befallen him would prevent the possibility of his being able to be present at the dinner he was giving that evening.

Day closed in and found the sky covered with heavy clouds. Towards eight o'clock a violent storm of rain fell, and when Carne heard it beating upon the deck above his cabin, and reflected that in consequence the night would in all probability be dark, he felt that his lucky star was indeed in the ascendant.

At half-past eight he retired to his cabin with Belton, in order to prepare for the events of the evening. Never before had he paid such careful attention to his make-up. He knew that on this occasion the least carelessness might lead to detection, and he had no desire that his last and greatest exploit should prove his undoing.

It was half-past nine before he and his servant had dressed and were ready to set off. Then, placing broad-brimmed hats upon their heads, and carrying a portmanteau containing the cloaks and headgear which they were to wear later in the evening, they went on deck and descended into the dinghy which was waiting for them alongside. In something under a quarter of an hour they had been put ashore in a secluded spot, had changed their costumes, and were walking boldly down beside the water towards the steps where they could see the Imperial launch still waiting. Her crew were lolling about, joking and laughing, secure in the knowledge that it would be some hours at least before their Sovereign would be likely to require their services again.

Their astonishment, therefore, may well be imagined when

they saw approaching them the two men whom they had only half an hour before brought ashore. Stepping in and taking his seat under the shelter, his Majesty ordered them to convey him back to the yacht with all speed. The accent and voice were perfect, and it never for an instant struck any one on board the boat that a deception was being practised. Carne, however, was aware that this was only a preliminary; the most dangerous portion of the business was yet to come.

On reaching the yacht, he sprang out on the ladder, followed by his aide-de-camp, Von Walzburg, and mounted the steps. His disguise must have been perfect indeed, for when he reached the deck he found himself face to face with the first lieutenant, who, on seeing him, saluted respectfully. For a moment Carne's presence of mind almost deserted him; then, seeing that he was not discovered, he determined upon a bold piece of bluff. Returning the officer's salute with just the air he had seen the Emperor use, he led him to suppose that he had important reasons for coming on board so soon, and, as if to back this assertion up, bade him send the chief steward to his cabin, and at the same time have the sentry removed from his door and placed at the end of the large saloon, with instructions to allow no one to pass until he was communicated with again.

The officer saluted and went off on his errand, while Carne, signing to Belton to follow him, made his way down the companion ladder to the Royal cabins. To both the next few minutes seemed like hours. Reaching the Imperial state room, they entered it and closed the door behind. Provided the sentry obeyed his orders, which there was no reason to doubt he would do, and the Emperor himself did not return until they were safely off the vessel again, there seemed every probability of their being able to carry out their scheme without a hitch.

"Put those bags under the table, and unwind the lines and place them in the gallery outside the window. They won't be seen there," said Carne to Belton, who was watching him from the doorway. "Then stand by, for in a few minutes the chief steward will be here. As soon as he enters you must manage to get between him and the door, and, while I am engaging him in conversation, spring on him, clutch him by the throat, and hold him until I can force this gag into his mouth. After that we shall be safe for some time at least, for not a soul will come this way until they discover their mistake. It seems to me we ought to thank our stars that the chief steward's cabin was placed in such a convenient position. But hush, here comes the individual we want. Be ready to collar him as soon as I hold up my hand. If he makes a sound we are lost."

He had scarcely spoken before there was a knock at the door. When it opened, the chief steward entered the cabin, closing the door behind him.

"Schmidt," said his Majesty, who was standing at the further end of the cabin, "I have sent for you in order that I may question you on a matter of the utmost importance. Draw nearer."

The man came forward as he was ordered, and, having done so, looked his master full and fair in the face. Something he saw there seemed to stagger him. He glanced at him a second time, and was immediately confirmed in his belief.

"You are not the Emperor," he cried. "There is some treachery in this. I shall call for assistance."

He had half turned, and was about to give the alarm, when Carne held up his hand, and Belton, who had been creeping stealthily up behind him, threw himself upon him and had clutched him by the throat before he could utter a sound. The fictitious Emperor immediately produced a cleverly constructed gag and forced it into the terrified man's mouth, who in another second was lying upon the floor bound hand and foot.

"There, my friend," said Carne quietly, as he rose to his feet a few moments later, "I don't think you will give us any further trouble. Let me just see that those straps are tight enough, and then we'll place you on this settee, and afterwards get to business with all possible dispatch."

Having satisfied himself on these points, he signed to Belton, and between them they placed the man upon the couch.

"Let me see, I think, if I remember rightly, you carry the key of the safe in this pocket."

So saying, he turned the man's pocket inside out and appropriated the bunch of keys he found therein. Choosing one from
it, he gave a final look at the bonds which secured the prostrate figure, and then turned to Belton.

"I think he'll do," he said. "Now for business. Bring the
bags, and come with me."

So saying, he crossed the cabin, and, having assured himself
that there was no one about to pry upon them, passed along
the luxuriously carpeted alley way until he arrived at the door
of the cabin, assigned to the use of the chief steward, and in
which was the safe containing the magnificent gold plate, the
obtaining of which was the reason of his being there. To his
surprise and chagrin, the door was closed and locked. In his
plans he had omitted to allow for this contingency. In all probability, however, the key was in the man's pocket, so, turning
to Belton, he bade him return to the state room and bring him
the keys he had thrown upon the table.

The latter did as he was ordered, and, when he had disappeared, Carne stood alone in the alley way waiting and listen-
ing to the various noises of the great vessel. On the deck
overhead he could hear some one tramping heavily up and
down, and then, in an interval of silence, the sound of pouring
rain. Good reason as he had to be anxious, he could not help
smiling as he thought of the incongruity of his position. He
wondered what his aristocratic friends would say if he were
captured and his story came to light. In his time he had impersonated a good many people, but never before had he had the
honour of occupying such an exalted station. This was the last
and most daring of all his adventures.

Minutes went by, and as Belton did not return, Carne found
himself growing nervous. What could have become of him?
He was in the act of going in search of him, when he appeared
carrying in his hand the bunch of keys for which he had been
sent. His master seized them eagerly.

"Why have you been so long?" he asked in a whisper. "I
began to think something had gone wrong with you."

"I stayed to make our friend secure," the other answered.
"He had well-nigh managed to get one of his hands free. Had

he done so, he would have had the gag out of his mouth in no time, and have given the alarm. Then we should have been caught like rats in a trap."

"Are you quite sure he is secure now?" asked Carne anxiously.

"Quite," replied Belton. "I took good care of that."

"In that case we had better get to work on the safe without further delay. We have wasted too much time already, and every moment is an added danger."

Without more ado, Carne placed, the most likely key in the lock and turned it. The bolt shot back, and the treasure chamber lay at his mercy.

The cabin was not a large one, but it was plain that every precaution had been taken to render it secure. The large safe which contained the Imperial plate, and which it was Carne's intention to rifle, occupied one entire side. It was of the latest design, and when Carne saw it he had to confess to himself that, expert craftsman as he was, it was one that would have required all his time and skill to open.

With the master key, however, it was the work of only a few seconds. The key was turned, the lever depressed, and then, with a slight pull, the heavy door swung forward. This done, it was seen that the interior was full to overflowing. Gold and silver plate of all sorts and descriptions, inclosed in bags of wash-leather and green baize, were neatly arranged inside. It was a haul such as even Carne had never had at his mercy before, and, now that he had got it, he was determined to make the most of it.

"Come, Belton," he said, "get these things out as quickly as possible and lay them on the floor. We can only carry away a certain portion of the plunder, so let us make sure that that portion is the best."

A few moments later the entire cabin was strewn with salvers, goblets, bowls, epergnes, gold and silver dishes, plates, cups, knives, forks, and almost every example of the goldsmith's art. In his choice Carne was not guided by what was handsomest or most delicate in workmanship or shape. Weight was his only standard. Silver he discarded altogether, for it was of less than no account. In something under ten minutes he had made his selection, and the stout canvas bags they had brought with them for that purpose were full to their utmost holding capacity.

"We can carry no more," said Carne to his faithful retainer, as they made the mouth of the last bag secure. "Pick up yours, and let us get back to the Emperor's state room.

Having locked the door of the cabin, they returned to the place whence they had started. There they found the unfortunate steward lying just as they had left him on the settee. Placing the bags he carried upon the ground, Carne crossed to him, and, before doing anything else, carefully examined the bonds with which he was secured.

Having done this, he went to the stern windows, and, throwing one open, stepped into the gallery outside. Fortunately for what he intended to do, it was still raining heavily, and in consequence the night was as dark as the most consummate conspirator could have desired. Returning to the room, he bade Belton help him carry the bags into the gallery, and, when this had been done, made fast the swivel hooks to the rings in the mouth of each.

"Take up your bags as quietly as possible," he said, "and lower them one by one into the water, but take care that they don't get entangled in the propeller. When you've done that, slip the rings at the other end of the lines through your belt, and buckle the latter tightly."

Belton did as he was ordered, and in a few moments the six bags were lying at the bottom of the sea.

"Now off with these wigs and things, and say when you're ready for a swim."

Their disguises having been discarded and thrown overboard, Carne and Belton clambered over the rails of the gallery and lowered themselves until their feet touched the water. Next moment they had both let go, and were swimming in the direction of Carne's own yacht.

It was at this period of their adventure that the darkness proved of such real service to them. By the time they had swum half a dozen strokes it would have needed a sharp pair of eyes to distinguish them as they rose and fell among the foam-crested waves. If, however, the storm had done them a good turn in saving them from notice, it came within an ace of doing them an ill service in another direction. Good swimmers though both Carne and Belton were, and they had proved it to each other's satisfaction in the seas of almost every known quarter of the globe, they soon found that it took all their strength to make headway now. By the time they reached their own craft, they were both completely exhausted. As Belton declared afterwards, he felt as if he could not have managed another twenty strokes even had his life depended on it.

At last, however, they reached the yacht's stern and clutched at the rope ladder which Carne had himself placed there before he had set out on the evening's excursion. In less time than it takes to tell, he had mounted it and gained the deck, followed by his faithful servant. They presented a sorry spectacle as they stood side by side at the taffrail, the water dripping from their clothes and pattering upon the deck.

"Thank goodness we are here at last," said Carne, as soon as he had recovered his breath sufficiently to speak. "Now slip off your belt, and hang it over this cleat with mine."

Belton did as he was directed, and then followed his master to the saloon companion ladder. Once below, they changed their clothes as quickly as possible, and having donned mackintoshes, returned to the deck, where it was still raining hard.

"Now," said Carne, "for the last and most important part of our evening's work. Let us hope the lines will prove equal to the demands we are about to make upon them."

As he said this, he took one of the belts from the cleat upon which he had placed it, and, having detached a line, began to pull it in, Belton following his example with another. Their hopes that they would prove equal to the confidence placed in them proved well founded, for, in something less than a quarter of an hour, the six bags, containing the Emperor of Westphalia's magnificent gold plate, were lying upon the deck, ready to be carried below and stowed away in the secret place in which Carne had arranged to hide his treasure.

"Now, Belton," said Carne, as he pushed the panel back

into its place, and pressed the secret spring that locked it, "I hope you're satisfied with what we have done. We've made a splendid haul, and you shall have your share of it. In the meantime, just get me to bed as quickly as you can, for I'm dead tired. When you've done so, be off to your own. To-morrow morning you will have to go up to town to arrange with the bank authorities about my account."

Belton did as he was ordered, and half an hour later his master was safely in bed and asleep.

It was late next morning when he woke. He had scarcely breakfasted before the Earl of Amberley and Lord Orpington made their appearance over the side. To carry out the part he had arranged to play, he received them seated in his deck chair, his swaddled up right foot reclining on a cushion before him. On seeing his guests, he made as if he would rise, but they begged him to remain seated.

"I hope your ankle is better this morning," said Lord Orpington politely, as he took a chair beside his friend.

"Much better, thank you," Carne replied. "It was not nearly so serious as I feared. I hope to be able to hobble about a little this afternoon. And now tell me the news, if there is any."

"Do you mean to say that you have not heard the great news?" asked Lord Amberley, in a tone of astonishment.

"I have heard nothing," Carne replied. "Remember, I have not been ashore this morning, and I have been so busily engaged with the preparations for my departure to-morrow that I have not had time to look at my papers. Pray what is this news of which you speak with such bated breath?"

"Listen, and I'll tell you," Lord Orpington answered. "As you are aware, last night his Imperial Majesty the Emperor of Westphalia dined ashore, taking with him his aide-de-camp, Count Von Walzburg. They had not been gone from the launch more than half an hour when, to all intents and purposes, they reappeared, and the Emperor, who seemed much perturbed about something, gave the order to return to the yacht with all possible speed. It was very dark and raining hard at the time, and whoever the men may have been who did the thing, they were, at any rate, past masters in the art of disguise.

"Reaching the yacht, their arrival gave rise to no suspicion, for the officers are accustomed, as you know, to his Majesty's rapid comings and goings. The first lieutenant met them at the gangway, and declares that he had no sort of doubt but that it was his Sovereign. Face, voice, and manner were alike perfect. From his Majesty's behaviour he surmised that there was some sort of trouble brewing for somebody, and, as if to carry this impression still further, the Emperor bade him send the chief steward to him at once, and, at the same time, place the sentry, who had hitherto been guarding the treasure chamber, at the end of the great saloon, with instructions to allow no one to pass him, on any pretext whatever, until the chief steward had been examined and the Emperor himself gave permission. Then he went below to his cabin.

"Soon after this the steward arrived, and was admitted. Something seems to have excited the latter's suspicions, however, and he was about to give the alarm when he was seized from behind, thrown upon the floor, and afterwards gagged and bound. It soon became apparent what object the rascals had in view. They had caused the sentry at the door of the treasure chamber to be removed and placed where not only he could not hinder them in their work, but would prevent them from being disturbed. Having obtained the key of the room and safe from the chief steward's pocket, they set off to the cabin, ransacked it completely, and stole all that was heaviest and most valuable of his Majesty's wonderful plate from the safe."

"Good gracious!" said Carne. "I never heard of such a thing. Surely it's the most impudent robbery that has taken place for many years past. To represent the Emperor of Westphalia and his aide-de-camp so closely that they could deceive even the officers of his own yacht, and to take a sentry off one post and place him in such a position as to protect them while at their own nefarious work, seems to me the very height of audacity. But how did they get their booty and themselves away again? Gold plate, under the most favourable circumstances, is by no means an easy thing to carry."

As he asked this question, Carne lit another cigar with a hand as steady as a rock.

"They must have escaped in a boat that, it is supposed, was lying under the shelter of the stern gallery," replied Lord Amberley.

"And is the chief steward able to furnish the police with no clue as to their identity?"

"None whatever," replied Orpington. "He opines to the belief, however, that they are Frenchmen. One of them, the man who impersonated the Emperor, seems to have uttered an exclamation in that tongue."

"And when was the robbery discovered?"

"Only when the real Emperor returned to the vessel shortly after midnight. There was no launch to meet him, and he had to get Tremorden to take him off. You can easily imagine the surprise his arrival occasioned. It was intensified when they went below to find his Majesty's cabin turned upside down, the chief steward lying bound and gagged upon the sofa, and all that was most valuable of the gold plate missing."

"What an extraordinary story!"

"And now, having told you the news with which the place is ringing, we must be off about our business," said Orpington. "Is it quite certain that you are going to leave us to-morrow?"

"Quite, I am sorry to say," answered Carne. "I am going to ask as many of my friends as possible to do me the honour of lunching with me at one o'clock, and at five I shall weigh anchor and bid England good-bye. I shall have the pleasure of your company, I hope."

"I shall have much pleasure," said Orpington.

"And I also," replied Amberley.

"Then good-bye for the present. It's just possible I may see you again during the afternoon."

The luncheon next day was as brilliant a social gathering as the most fastidious in such matters could have desired. Every one then in Cowes who had any claim to distinction was present, and several had undertaken the journey from town in order to say farewell to one who had made himself so popular during his brief stay in England. When Carne rose to reply to the toast of his health, proposed by the Prime Minister, it was observable that he was genuinely moved, as, indeed, were most of his hearers.

For the remainder of the afternoon his yacht's deck was crowded with his friends, all of whom expressed the hope that it might not be very long before he was amongst them once more.

To these kind speeches Carne invariably offered a smiling reply.

"I also trust it will not be long," he answered. "I have enjoyed my visit immensely, and you may be sure I shall never forget it as long as I live."

An hour later the anchor was weighed, and his yacht was steaming out of the harbour amid a scene of intense enthusiasm. As the Prime Minister had that afternoon informed him, in the public interest, the excitement of his departure was dividing the honours with the burglary of the Emperor of Westphalia's gold plate.

Carne stood beside his captain on the bridge, watching the little fleet of yachts until his eyes could no longer distinguish them. Then he turned to Belton, who had just joined him, and, placing his hand upon his shoulder, said:

"So much for our life in England, Belton, my friend. It has been glorious fun, and no one can deny that from a business point of view it has been eminently satisfactory. You, at least, should have no regrets."

"None whatever," answered Belton. "But I must confess I should like to know what they will say when the truth comes out."

Carne smiled sweetly as he answered:

"I think they'll say that, all things considered, I have won the right to call myself 'A Prince of Swindlers.'"